WITHIN THE NO RETURN

And there, at opposite edges of the clearing were pieces
of the puzzle that he had been chasing for days. The
grizzly bear was on one side of the clearing, not fifty
yards away from where he stood. Although Doug must
have clearly been within range of its senses, it paid
him no heed, for it had found its original target, that
which stood on the opposite side of the clearing.

Doug quickly moved behind the visual protection of a
mass of boulders before he got a good look across the
way. He ducked behind the largest boulder, and
placed his back against it. Fear was coursing through
his veins, and he was visibly shaking, his shotgun was
vibrating in his trembling hands. The dark visions of
the previous two nights assaulted his psyche like a
whiplash. It took all of his courage to tilt his head to
the side, and peek around the boulder.

Doug could see the large humanoid through a gap in
the trees...

NO RETURN

a novel by
Pete Travers

The Painted Cave Publishing
Santa Barbara, CA

Copyright © 2006 The Painted Cave
Cover design by Pete Travers

The Painted Cave
P.O. Box 6587, Santa Barbara, CA 93160

Visit our website at:
www.thepaintedcave.com

A PAINTED CAVE™ BOOK
Painted Cave Books are published by The Painted Cave

Publisher's Cataloging-in-Publication
(Provided by Quality Books, Inc.)

Travers, Pete, 1971-
    No return : a novel / by Pete Travers.
    p. cm.
    LCCN 2004096904
    ISBN-13: 978-0-9748698-4-1
    ISBN-10: 0-9748698-4-8

    1. Sasquatch--Fiction. 2. Wilderness areas--Idaho--Fiction. 3. Fathers and sons--Fiction. 4. Hunting--Idaho--Fiction. 5. Idaho--Fiction. 6. Adventure fiction. I. Title.

PS3620.R38N6 2006   813'.6
                             QBI05-600201

PRINTED IN THE UNITED STATES OF AMERICA

10 9 8 7 6 5 4 3 2 1

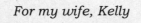

For my wife, Kelly

PROLOGUE

Idaho 1853
(as told by Teddy Roosevelt)[1]

Two men on horseback entered a pass in the vast wilderness of the Idaho Territories. Bauman, a pure-blood frontiersman, and his hunting partner, White, rode through the shaded gap observing the quiet still of the dark woods around them. They could see the brighter light ahead, baiting them through the dense forest of pine. It was not long before they cleared the shadowed pass and stopped at an outcropping of rock, balanced high above a wide expanse of dropping terrain. Ahead of them, a river lay across the bottom of a pristine valley. In the early sunshine, golden rays cast down on the small tributary reflecting an image of flowing gold through an emerald green landscape. To the men, it was a symbol for a prosperous future.

A couple of weeks back, Bauman had received a tip from a fellow trapper in Boise that there was a valley

---

[1] Adapted from *The Wilderness Hunter*

between the Snake and Salmon Rivers of Idaho which had game hunting like no other. The only problem, he had said, was that it was haunted, and even the Indians didn't go there. The valley, it was said, was steeped in an evil reputation. But Bauman and White were un-phased by the lore, for they were far too experienced to be scared away by tall tales. Besides, there was so much game in the area, especially beaver, which would provide good money in Boise. It had been a hard winter, and it was necessary to take advantage of the springtime, when the beaver were more active, and therefore, easier to trap. So the hunters made their way into the valley and set up camp by the riverbed.

The hunting was very prosperous that first day. Traps were set down along a three-mile length of the river. In the bright midday sunshine, Bauman sat in the tall grass by the riverbed and watched as the beaver made their way fearlessly toward the set traps. Bauman was amazed at how easily the beavers could be caught.

Bauman felt that this might prove as bountiful a trip as he had enjoyed in a long time. The valley was an aberration. It was a pristine place, like men had never set foot there before. And Bauman could only feel lucky to find a place such as this in the days of the rapidly dwindling frontier.

As the day followed on however, Bauman was getting a strange feeling like he was being watched. But having not seen nor heard anything unusual, he did not mention it to White. Still, as time passed through the slow day, he could not shake the nagging sensation of eyes upon him. The men retired back to camp at sundown, their packs full of pelts.

When they arrived at their camp, they realized that something had ransacked their belongings. Also, the horses were a distance away, rustled away from their original grazing spot, spooked about something. It had made the men somewhat uneasy, for though they had lived in the wilderness for many years, neither one could remember having their camp messed up in such a strange manner. Whatever it was that had bothered the camp was after more than food, for all of the belongings had been disturbed, not just the food packs.

Bauman found the situation peculiar. White had initially guessed that a bear was the culprit, but dismissed it for bear only cared about one thing, food. Bears had a tremendous sense of smell, and they used it with extreme determination and focus, foraging only through those items that smelled of food. Whatever had bothered the camp had wanted to make a mess. The thing had even gone through the trapping gear. Had they disturbed the nest of some other kind of large animal?

White elected to search for animal sign. The ground consisted of hard packed earth around the immediate campsite, so he checked wider out by circling the perimeter and scanning the terrain. White was a superb tracksman, knowing all sign from bear to wolf to anything that lived in the North American forests.

But giving it twenty minutes, he determined that there was nothing to find. The hard ground of the campsite rolled into the packed needles fallen from the neighboring Douglas firs. If something wanted to walk softly, it could easily do so here. What White did notice was a faint pungent odor that seemed to emanate from all directions. It smelled like rotten garbage. But the smell could only be dismissed as a curiosity, for there were no tracks to be found, and therefore, no conclusions could be made.

The two men cleaned up and got ready for bed, and retired in their lean-to. The warm sun fell over the mountain ridge and the inevitable darkness crept over the sky. The tall flame of the campfire diminished to glowing embers and then to a smoky black pyre. The coldness from the higher elevations descended and became trapped in the lower recesses of the valley. The hunters fell asleep shortly after nightfall.

Sometime in the middle of the night, Bauman woke up to a noise. Looking out of the lean-to, a huge shape was eclipsing the moonlight, practically covering the entire opening of the refuge. Bauman, thinking it was a bear, pulled up his rifle right from the side of his bedding and fired point blank at the animal. The animal reacted and pulled back. It screamed as it retreated. It wasn't the speed of the animal that Bauman found the most disturbing, but rather the way it ran. It ran away on two legs, like a man.

His blood still pumping hard from the encounter, Bauman turned to see his partner wide-eyed and fully alert. White stated that he had seen the creature, for he had awoken before Bauman had fired the gun.

The unexpected visit made the hunters extremely uneasy. The animal had clearly run away in the moonlight on two legs. The thing was so large that you could hear the thundering footsteps even after the animal was out of sight. Neither man had seen nor heard anything like that in sixty combined years of being out in the deep wild.

Blasting howls emerged from the surrounding forest. White commented that it sounded like an elk, but more like a human yell and quite a bit more powerful.

Screams from the forest continued. On and on it went throughout the night, echoing off the valley walls. Hours rolled away and still the animal lingered.

White questioned his friend on whether he truly believed he had hit the animal, but Bauman assured him that he did hit the thing point blank. Bauman's assuredness however, did little to rest the fears of the two frontiersmen, as the screams in the night continued on. The animal, whether it was hurt or not, did not sound hurt. It sounded angry. Bauman began to understand why the Indians stayed away from this place.

A much closer noise split the night, not twenty feet away from the clearing. It sounded like breathing, but it was much louder, as if intentionally trying to attract attention. It was an even intake of air into what sounded like a very large set of lungs.

Bauman heard the noise and whispered to White for a confirmation that he had heard it as well. White answered by telling Bauman to not turn towards it. White wanted to surprise the animal. They agreed to turn and fire on the count of three, attempting to surprise the beast.

Both men turned and fired their rifles waist high towards the breathing. At twenty feet, it was an easy shot for either hunter. But in the flash of the rifle fire, all they could see was the tree line.

Just then, on the opposite side of camp, deeper into the woods, a loud scream blasted the silence.

The two men were baffled by the speed of the creature. Nothing could move that fast.

White aimed his rifle in the direction of the new sound and fired a blast towards it. He angled slightly to the left and fired and then to the right and fired again, hoping to catch the animal in movement.

Another loud snap of a tree branch not fifty yards away cut his hopes down.

Bauman immediately searched his memory of what the trapper from Boise had told him about this place. The fellow had said that the valley was haunted. Bauman originally thought that he meant that the valley was haunted by old Indian spirits, or something of that nature. But looking back on it, he remembered the fellow specifically saying something about the Nez Perce, the local Indians, staying well clear of this place. The Indians didn't get scared about their own people's spirits. It wasn't like them. But something kept them away from this place. *Smart move,* he thought. Bauman had been in the woods a long time, and it was a rarity that he would ever be spooked about anything. Sure, grizzly were something to be very concerned about, but they were predictable. They wanted food, and if they were real hungry, they would try to make you into a meal. But this was different. This was no animal he had ever heard of, with behavior he had never seen before. He wasn't sure if it was even an animal. It ran away on two legs. Grizzlies can walk on two legs, but he had never seen one run without being on all fours.

The sounds continued, but they were getting more distant as time went by.

Bauman and White had decided to take shifts sleeping, one staying awake to stand guard. Yet with the creature's chilling screams in the distance, it was enough that neither man got any sleep for the rest of the night. It was the strangest noise, something between a deathly scream and a powerful roar. Bauman could not remember a time when he wished more that a night would end. The screams spiraled away, always emanating from a new place in the valley, circling higher and higher towards the valley ridge. By focusing on the screams, Bauman noticed that the forest was absolutely silent, absent of the usual nightly sounds to which he was accustomed. The lack of noise between screams made the night even more eerie.

Time passed. Bauman could feel the moisture in the air. Dew was settling on the tall grass around him. The stars arced through the night sky. Hours rolled by as the sky faded to a hazy blue, then orange from the east. As tired as he should have been, he could not feel the urges of sleep. Instinctively, his mind went into survival mode, staying alert, listening to the sounds of the forest. Over the next few hours, the customary noises of the woods returned, and then came the sounds of birds, chirping in the trees, heralding the new day.

Dawn finally broke. The men agreed to stick together during the day. They figured they would cover less ground, but it seemed appropriate considering last night's events.

As the sun emerged over the valley ridge, their fears slowly ebbed away and the two enjoyed another great day of trapping in the bright and warm springtime sun. They traveled together up and down the length of the tributary, checking and setting traps as they went along.

White could not believe the ease at which the hunting and trapping progressed. It was almost as if the animals did not even try to avoid their human assailants. Bauman agreed and counted his pelts at six, with White's four making a total of ten adult beaver in one day. They could not remember a yield that robust ever in their trapping days in the West. Ten beaver would ordinarily take a week to trap. *Maybe no one came here,* Bauman thought. That was why the animals were not scared of them.

White questioned whether *it* ate beaver. Bauman was glad that they hadn't talked about *it* for a while. The peacefulness of the day was in stark contrast to the night. Bauman did not know what the thing ate, but it had plenty of food supply if it ate meat.

And White wanted to take all of it. He was not accustomed to being out of his element. The valley got under his skin and he wanted to take his anxiety out on the wildlife. Bauman understood his frustration and even his fear of the unknown, for it was fear that White did not want to show. Bauman insisted that they had enough pelts for the summer, and that they should leave first thing on the morrow.

White responded negatively with bravado, but Bauman knew better. White was a stubborn fellow. If White really wanted to stick around, he would have made a stronger argument. His lack of enthusiasm for staying was a clear indication that last night's events had bothered him more than he wanted to admit.

By day's end, without incident, the hunters made their way back to camp. Bauman, however, remembered some traps he had forgotten down near the opposite end of the river valley. He believed that there were about four traps. He had set them just past the rapids they had found in the morning.

The separation would have broken the pact they had made earlier, but without incident during the day, they assured themselves that a quick trip up the river alone was not much of a risk. White insisted that Bauman go and get the traps while he prepared dinner. Bauman agreed and said he would be back in twenty minutes.

The two split up and went in opposite directions on horseback.

Bauman followed the river up stream, meandering through the valley. Since there were no offshoots of the tributary in this area, it was very easy to find his way, so he moved at a half gallop along the waterline. In a few minutes, he passed by the rapids where the river narrowed and became increasingly shallow. The traps were set right at the sandy edge of the water in the side pools where the water slowed. To his surprise, three of the four traps were sprung. More incredible odds. Beaver weren't particularly fond of rapids, preferring the slow moving channels where they could build their dams, but these pools were big enough and deep enough that they might attract the animals. And the attraction went well beyond what Bauman would have expected. Bauman wondered if this was what it was like in the early days of the frontier, a beaver family in every river, a group of elk in every forest, and a herd of buffalo in every field. It was like that once, no more than a hundred years ago, but things had changed when men, like him, came to these places. And as more and more white men reached into the West, the tougher it was to make a living as a trapper.

Somehow, the Indians did it right, he thought, and we took it away from them. They managed to live in these territories for centuries without over-fishing and hunting them. Bauman had learned the trade from his father, a great hunter and trapper in his time. But Bauman remembered that his father became disenchanted with hunting in the frontier as time went on, mainly because of what happened to the Indians. The United States government had put a steep price on the killing of the buffalo, not because of the value of the fur, but because of the impact on the Indian. The leaders of the U.S. government, as virtuous as they sounded when defending the rights and freedom of man, did not think much of the red skinned folk. As a matter of fact, they wanted them to all die, he thought. That's why they ordered for the destruction of the buffalo, which was the main life source of a large portion of native tribes. Frontiersmen were paid good money to kill as many buffalo as they could find. As valuable as the furs were to sell, the hunters left them and grabbed the horns, because it was a faster way to show the proof of their kills. The plains were cleared of the migrating herds of bison within a few years. As the buffalo were wiped out, those Indians tribes that were at one with nature, faded away as well. The Nez Perce were all but gone from the central Idaho territories. Only the legacy of their names remained.

But Bauman, as regretful as he was, had to make a

living. And trapping was the skill he knew best. He tried to not overtrap, but it forced him and White to trek to more remote regions and have a broader area to travel across. Bauman didn't mind however, for it gave him a chance to see the still primal areas of the uncharted frontier, as it must have once looked. This place was one of them, a valley from the past, from a time before the white man.

Bauman cleared the traps and packed them. He then took the kills and slung them over his horse. He usually did the skinning right then and there, but he wanted to get back to camp. He got on his horse and headed off with plenty of light still left in the day.

Bauman followed the river back. On his approach to the campsite, he became alarmed. The camp had been invaded again, as pots and furs were strewn about. There was no movement, other than the lightweight supplies blowing around in the breeze. He then caught sight of his partner, sitting by a tree stump, not moving.

Bauman yelled ahead to White, but he couldn't get his attention. He moved closer.

A strange rush went over his bones as he noticed his partner's face struck in fear, his neck clearly broken to one side. His eyes and mouth were wide open in a ghastly pose. White was dead.

Just then, a bellowing scream blasted through the woods. It echoed throughout the valley, so much that he could not determine its direction. Bauman made a complete circle, looking around, seeing nothing. But it was there and it was close. Bauman quickly jumped back on his horse, so afraid that he rode at full gallop out of the camp, leaving everything, including White, behind. He blasted through the woods at breakneck speed. The trees and brush were slapping him and his horse as they climbed, but Bauman could not even feel it. He kept looking back. His common sense told him that nothing in the woods could outrun a horse at full gallop, but his instincts told him that something was close, as if it was all around him. As he rode higher and higher towards the valley ridge, he passed by a dark shape with outstretched arms. Moving so fast he did not even see it until the last moment. He almost fell from his horse when he saw it, thinking it was the creature that had killed White. But it was not moving, stuck in its frozen stance, facing away from the valley. The low sun silhouetted the giant shape. Bauman was too afraid to stop and get a closer look, for fear of being attacked in the dense trees.

Bauman rode on. He kept riding hard until he cleared the trees, breaking into the higher altitudes above the timberline. The horse was frothing at the mouth from the exertion of the uphill gallop. Bauman did not look back anymore. He rode away over the valley ridge and beyond, never to return again.

Bauman imparted his story to a young Theodore Roosevelt, future captain of the Rough Riders and

President of the United States. Roosevelt always believed that Bauman was an honest man, and of sound judgment, and even accompanied him on an excursion or two. Roosevelt relayed Bauman's story in one of his memoirs. But as time passed, it became dismissed as another tall tale from the frontier.

CHAPTER ONE

Present Day

Doug Childress and his friend, Evan Ratcliffe, sat in a bar named *Hair of the Dog*. The bar was located in a small town called Omah, about 100 miles northeast of Boise, Idaho. Omah was a frontier town, founded in the early 1800's for the fur and gem trade. It was situated along Highway 21, now known as the Ponderosa Pine Scenic Biway. The road had served as the main thoroughfare for trekking between two great wilderness areas, the Sawtooth Mountains to the south and the No Return Wilderness to the north.

The *Hair of the Dog* was what used to be an old stagecoach stop, a place to rest for wayward travelers making the long trek from Boise into the Idaho Panhandle and on to Canada. The bar was a log cabin, complete with mounted animal heads of deer, elk and bear. It made for a comfortable favorite hangout for the locals. On a Thursday night, there were few patrons, but the place was rarely empty. Omah had little to do at night, and Boise was too far of a drive. Having a population of approximately ten thousand with little growth, Omah had few options.

The warm atmosphere of the bar, however offered a place to wind down and talk about whatever came to mind. Doug and Evan made a habit of meeting on Thursday nights. They sat at their usual spot, at the end of the twenty foot long heavily shellacked bar that was made of one piece of a giant fir tree. The barstools as well were each made from a single piece of timber. The two men each drank from a sixteen-ounce glass of tap beer.

Doug was a very average looking man, with medium height, a slight build and decent looks. Doug worked at a local bank as a financial consultant. He grew up in Tacoma Washington, but his family moved out to rural Idaho, desiring to get away from it all. He, however, did not have the same desires. First chance he got, he went away. Doug studied finance at Boise State University, but he was not a stellar student. His drive to succeed could never overcome his own complacency. In his senior year in college, he met his wife, Ellen. She was also from a small town in central Idaho, but did not mind it as much as Doug. They returned to Ellen's hometown of Omah, got married and had a son. Doug's career had to be achieved within the tiny confines of a small town, in which his job consisted primarily of giving advice to farmers on where they should channel their money, or as was more often the case, their lack of money. He looked out of place in the rustic bar with a suit on, especially next to Evan.

Evan was of stronger build, and had the look of an outdoorsman, with thick hands and forearms, and semi-clean clothes made mostly of denim. He was a local contract carpenter, and mostly dealt in repair work for people's homes. He had lived in Omah for most of his life, moving to Idaho from Boulder, Colorado as a young teenager. Evan loved it here and always felt at home in the wide landscape of the American West. They were a strange pair with contrasting interests, but they had become good friends nonetheless. Both men were in their late thirties.

The two men stared at their beers as if something was important inside them. Doug asked Evan for advice on what to do this Labor Day weekend with his fourteen-year-old son, Chad.

"I don't want to do anything that's gonna get the kid bored. What would a fourteen-year-old kid want to do for a whole weekend, besides hang out with girls?"

Doug was divorced, had been so for about a year, and this was the first time that he would get to be with his son for a three-day weekend, so he wanted to do something special.

"Well, what do you want to do?" Evan said.

"I don't know." Doug replied.

It seemed to be a ritual for their conversations. Evan

was the decision maker, even if it was Doug's decision to make. Doug was not the decisive type. He preferred to let others work through his own problems. Evan ultimately did not mind his role, figuring it was always easier to solve other people's problems than one's own. Evan would just prod the conversation along until Doug came to the appropriate predestined decision.

"Do you want to do an outdoorsy kind of thing?"

"Maybe." Doug responded.

Evan told him, "There's a place near the Salmon River in the No Return Wilderness, where the hunting is amazing, and no one goes there because it's right on the edge of an area the Indians considered sacred. I mean, it's some of the best turkey hunting you'll find. I swear, I think this place is where the expression *turkey shoot* comes from. You cannot miss."

Doug could not relate because he had never been hunting before, or even true camping for that matter. Doug never had the taste for being outdoors like Evan did. Evan frequently offered for Doug to join him on hunting trips, but Doug always declined, not necessarily because he didn't want to go, but because he never had the energy for it. But now, for some reason, it sounded a lot more appealing with Chad being involved. "How far is it?" Doug asked starting to like the idea.

"Not far at all, just a little ways outside of town, and

then down a fire road and you're there. The kid'll love it. Shooting shit and camping by the fire. Total man stuff."

"Ellen would hate it." Doug realized apprehensively.

"Who gives a shit what she thinks, Doug. For what she did to you, you do not owe her anything."

"Did you know that everybody at the bank knows about the divorce bullshit?"

"How did they found out?"

"Public record. They have to do personnel checks on anybody with higher security levels at a branch for my bank chain. So I figured my manager must have seen it and spread it to everybody. Thanks, dickhead."

Doug finished off his beer.

"That sucks man." Evan consoled Doug and then decided, "You should have fought it."

"Well, I can't Evan." Doug explained. "It's on my record, he didn't conjure it up."

"No. I mean you should have fought it during the divorce. It's total bullshit."

Doug sat quiet for moment, following a familiar thread of thought. He had run it through many times and always came to the same conclusion. "They wouldn't have believed me."

A moment of silence passed. Evan wanted to push the issue, to force Doug into action, but thought better of it. Doug had to get there on his own with this one.

Doug broke the silence. "Anyway, it hasn't changed my management status, but I don't think I am going to have too much upward mobility at the bank. Maybe I'll quit or something and work at a credit union. They are pretty lax, I heard."

Evan changed the subject. "Speaking of lax, you should just think about the weekend, man. You are going to have a blast out there. No one goes out there, so you'll just have the peace and quiet to share with Chad."

"Yeah, it sounds like a lot of fun." He nodded. "And I think Chad will like it."

Doug looked at the wall behind the bar. It was covered with old photographs of men standing by their animal kills. He knew why Evan liked this place.

The obvious occurred to Doug. "Uhhh, one thing..." he paused. "I don't know how to hunt."

"Not to worry." Evan replied quickly. "Come over the house tomorrow, and I'll show you what you need to know. I can give you all of the supplies you will need, as well. But you'll have to get your own food."

"Oh, you sure you can't make some sandwiches for me or anything?" Doug quipped. Evan liked Doug's dry sense of humor.

Doug was excited. The two paid for their beers. On the way out, the bartender gave them back their keys, knowing that they only had two beers each.

"Oh shit, I almost forgot. Can you throw this in my account?" Evan asked as he tossed an envelope of cash towards Doug. Doug caught the envelope in mid-air as he was making his way to his SUV.

"Jesus Evan, do you always walk around with envelopes full of cash?"

"Nahh, it's just that Mrs. Keel refuses to write checks for anything, especially the roof job I'm doing for her. I think she has all her money buried underneath her house." Evan continued to walk towards his truck. "Thanks Doug. I'll see you tomorrow."

"Good night Evan." Doug climbed into his SUV and started the vehicle. He patted his chest, feeling his shirt pocket to make sure he had his bank keys with him, which he always carried separately from his car keys. He wasn't about to hand the keys for the town's only bank vault to a bartender.

He drove off toward the center of town. He arrived at the deserted bank, and used his security keys to open up the front door. He unlocked the vault, deposited the money, then went to one of the cashier's stations and left the deposit information for one of the clerk's to see in the morning. Tired and excited about the upcoming weekend, he quickly headed back home.

Doug stopped by Evan's house late the next morning. Evan was in the backyard, making an organized pile of items for Doug's trip.

"Now all you *really* need is some beer, hot dogs and a rifle, but I wanted to make sure you were prepared for anything. My boy's first day at camp." Evan made a pretend motherly gesture and tried to hug Doug.

"Get away from me." Doug laughed and backed away.

Evan went back in the house and got a pair of binoculars and what looked like a tent. "Now you can sleep in your car, or SUV, or whatever you call that thing, but just remember to keep the food away from yourself when you sleep."

"Why?" Doug asked.

"Bears." Evan flatly replied.

"Bears! You didn't tell me that bears were up there." Doug acted as if he had been lied to.

"You didn't ask. Now it'll be fine. They're pretty elusive. They are not like the bears in Yellowstone where they're used to finding food in garbage. These

guys are fairly passive, and don't really have a
habitual taste for human food. So, just play by the
rules and you'll be fine." Evan was talking to Doug
while he was looking over the pile of supplies.

"What are the rules?"

"Generally, make sure your food is tucked away. Now
it's not like where your going is an official campsite, so
you won't have a bear box."

"What's a bear box?"

"It's like a safe, but for food, but you won't have one so
it doesn't really matter. What you're going to do is
make your own."

"How do I do that?" Doug asked.

"Well I made a harness for your cooler, I mean my
cooler. It gets attached to a rope. You throw the rope
over a high branch, like so." Evan took the slack from
the rope and flung it over the large branch about ten
feet above him. The slack from the end of the rope
came down with a flop on the other side. "Pull the
cooler up to about 3 feet away from the branch and tie
the rope off on the trunk. Make the sure the branch is
at least fifteen feet high and clear of other foliage.
There is a perfect tree for this at the site. It's a
ponderosa pine about twenty feet from the fire pit.
You can't miss it. It has a really red trunk."

"What if a bear is tall enough to grab it?" Doug asked,

knowing the question sounded stupid.

"If a bear is tall enough to grab your food at fifteen feet high, you got other problems. Only the biggest of grizzlies could do that."

"Are there grizzlies in the No Return?"

"Yeah, but they are very, very rare. They are almost gone. Most of the grizzlies that you'll see in this state are way up in the Panhandle, near Glacier Park." Evan assured him.

"Evan, I don't know. You are making me nervous."

"Relax, I have been up there about twenty times and I have never seen a grizzly, or a black bear for that matter. They just don't come around. I'm just telling you this stuff so you and Chad can be super safe."

"What happens if I do see one?"

"Okay, here's the deal. Black bears and grizzly bears have entirely different behaviors, so you need to react differently. Remember the phrase 'black, don't crack'. What that means is that you don't back down from a black bear. Stand your ground and wave your arms at it and yell at it. They'll back away. Black bears don't get much bigger than two hundred pounds, so you have a size advantage."

"No I wouldn't, I'm one-eighty-five." Doug argued.

"Well, yeah." Evan made a dismissive gesture. "The point is that you're too big for a black bear to ever consider food."

"Right, what about grizzly?" Doug asked.

"The rule is 'grizz-lee, find a tree'. Slowly back away and find a tall tree to climb. Grizzly are terrible climbers. They are just too heavy. Try not to make eye contact with one. Oh, and don't run away from them either. That might instigate a chase reaction." Evan went on.

"Of course, why would I run away? That would seem foolish. When large carnivores are coming my way, I usually frolic away from them, singing a happy tune." Doug snorted.

Evan ignored him and changed the subject. "Okay, 'nother thing. Bring plenty of water. Bring a couple gallons of it. You're not going to be backpacking, so you can buy one of those big plastic jugs at the supermarket. Whatever you do, don't drink the river water."

"Why can't I drink the water?" Doug was holding up his hands.

"Because you may get very sick from it. There is a lot of bacteria in it. Some stuff can live in your stomach for years. Nasty shit called giardia. It'll give you diarrhea for life, and there's no cure."

"Nice. How come the animals don't get it?" Doug was envisioning a whole forest full of animals running around with bowel problems.

"Because they are immune. I could give you a water filter and purifier, but I'd rather you just bring your own water. Not to say that you might screw it up." Evan smiled.

"Thanks. You don't trust me with water, but you'll let me borrow your shotgun."

"Pretty much. Which is an excellent segway into our next topic: guns." Evan beckoned Doug over to the picnic table where a long shotgun and some red plastic shells were. "Alright, this a Remington 870 Autoloading Wingmaster."

"What, does it load itself?"

"No, it's just that after you fire it, the next shell will be ready--as opposed to a bolt-action."

"Ahh, got it." Doug acknowledged.

"So anyway, here's how you load it." Evan handed the shotgun to Doug as he talked him through it. "First, point the gun in a safe direction. Always a good idea. Now, engage the safety mechanism. That red band there on the trigger will not show, see it?"

"Yeah, I mean no. The red band is not showing." Doug relayed as he tilted the shotgun downward to get a closer look at the trigger area.

"Good." Evan continued. "Pull the operating handle fully rearward until the bolt is held open by the carrier latch. Put the shell in the ejection port, which is the hole right there on the side of the barrel. Good. Oh, and keep your fingers away from the operating handle. Yup. Push up on the carrier release to close the action. Now, put another shell into the magazine tube."

"How many can I put in?" Doug asked, getting the hang of it.

"Eight shells, but I hope you won't need it. So now, disengage the safety mechanism, and you're ready. Excellent. Okay, so now it's time to see how good of a shot you are. Aim for that tree over there, and make sure you have the stock up against your shoulder."

"Look through the scope?" Doug asked.

"Yeah, you can if you want. It's on a cantilever assembly, so you can pull it off to the side and look through the sight if you want. The thing with shotguns, as opposed to rifles, is that they aren't super accurate. They fire a spread of small pellets, and this one has a modified choke, which basically means its good from about sixty yards. If you hit anything past that range, I would be impressed."

"I'd be impressed if I hit anything within ten yards." Doug replied dryly.

Doug took a moment to line up the tree inside the gun scope. He figured it was about thirty yards away. He squeezed the trigger. The gun blasted with a very loud noise and the recoil of it was stronger than he would have expected, pushing his shoulder back.

He looked at the tree. A large chunk of bark was ripped away to the left of center.

"I hit it!"

"Yeah, not a direct hit, but pretty good for a first try."

Doug sighted the tree and fired again. This time the blast radius hit squarely on the trunk.

"Well done." Evan nodded.

Doug was beginning to like the idea of this trip again. The possibility of encountering a bear was really making him nervous, especially having Chad out there with him. But he guessed that that's how man stuff was supposed to be--nervous at first, but afterwards, a good story to tell, and maybe a little adventure.

"So, there's a blind set up about a quarter of a mile from camp. I'd suggest hanging out there for hunting. You could go through the woods looking for game, but you'll probably make too much noise trampling around and scare any game away. There's a trail at the far end of the camp. Follow it and it'll take you right to the blind."

"Got it."

"Well, those are the basics." Evan said. "The rest is small stuff. You can figure out how to put the tent up right?"

"Yeah, I can handle that. Hey, thanks Evan."

"No problem. I'll give you a hand with putting the gear in your car. Oh, and tell Chad I said hello."

"Will do. See ya in a couple of days."

In the afternoon, Doug drove to his ex-wife's house to pick up Chad. It had actually been Doug's house as well, but he had agreed to give it up during the divorce. It was a three-bedroom townhouse, right downtown in a back street neighborhood. Doug always liked the house. It was roomy and was situated in a nice way where a lot of natural light would come in during the day. He bought it before Chad was born, financing his own loan through the bank. He had watched the interest rates at work until they dropped really low during the eighties and refinanced, making the payments very affordable...very affordable for *her*. He was proud of the house, being that it was his first major purchase in life. And now, that was taken away from him, as well as Chad.

Nevertheless, Doug was in high spirits because he was

really looking forward to the weekend. It was going to be a good trip, a simple trip.

But his mood dropped back down when he saw Ellen at the doorway of the house. A million different thoughts and memories flashed through Doug's mind when he looked at her face. Ellen was pretty, by anybody's standards, and she had one of those faces that didn't age. She looked the same now as she did in her twenties. Yeah, she was beautiful. She would always be beautiful. No one could easily walk away from a life with a beauty like that. But the divorce was not his idea. It was hers. Doug felt that they could have worked it out, but Ellen refused to, and took Chad away from him in the process.

Doug and Ellen exchanged cold glances as Chad came out of the house alone. Chad seemed very distant on the surface, but was paying very close attention to his parents' interaction. He stood between them as if to try to bridge them together, so that they would talk, but they never did. They always talked through him now, never to each other directly. He had become their reluctant interpreter.

"Did you tell your mother that you would be back on Monday?" Doug asked Chad with Ellen obviously within earshot.

"Yeah Dad, I did." Chad replied in a tone that made it sound like it was a stupid question. This seemed to please Ellen.

"Don't do anything stupid, Chad. Come back in one piece." She walked over and gave Chad a warm hug.

Doug didn't even know what to say. It was a potshot at him. He knew it. But he wasn't going to bite by trying to reassure her that he would take care of Chad. It was pointless to attempt to make conversation with Ellen, and competing with her was even worse. She just didn't care about him anymore. A person who was once his best friend in the whole world, the one he trusted more than anyone else, had become his enemy. Someone who hated him. His life had become much worse for it as well.

Doug and Chad climbed into the SUV. As he pulled away, Doug looked in the rear view mirror at Ellen standing on the front lawn.

His front lawn.

Pete Travers

CHAPTER TWO

Doug drove the SUV down the main street of Omah. The old town stores drifted past, looking like postcards from long ago. Omah had become a tourist town in the last ten years, or at least it was trying to. The tourism trade was just not thriving, for the town possessed little historical significance, compared to the more famous communities, like Idaho City to the south. He knew of a few friends and families who had tried their turn at renting the high priced property in old town to open up trinket shops, but none of them were successful. There just weren't enough tourists. Most visitors that came through Omah were on their way to rafting on the north fork of the Salmon. In the end, the renters would have to close up shop, because they would run out of money. What bothered Doug the most was that the owners of the property lived in Boise or other places, but not here. They would just charge high rents from afar, have a high turnover rate, but not really feel the effects of stripping these hopeful shopkeepers out of their money.

They stopped at a local strip mall and parked in front of the only major supermarket in town. Doug grabbed a shopping cart. When his hands touched the cart handle, a memory flashed through his mind.

He thought of when he used to go shopping with Chad on Saturdays. Chad was only about two years old at the time. Doug had enjoyed running errands on the weekends, for it gave him an opportunity to wind down and accomplish something at the same time. The weeks weren't terribly strenuous at the bank, but it was tiring to deal with so many people during the span of a week. The majority of the customers were having some kind of problem with their money, and he had to hear it. Fridays were always the worst. People tried to blast through during lunch hour to cash their weekly paychecks, making for huge lines of high anxiety customers. Combine that with when the stock market tanked, and work was almost unbearable. That's why it was so fun to hang out with Chad on the weekends. He used to sit there in the carriage seat, happy as can be. Customers at work were upset when their mutual fund would drop a point, but Chad was completely entertained by riding in a shopping cart. Doug always remembered the look that Chad would give him. His son never looked around to see where the cart was going. He just looked at Dad. Doug would drive the cart around all the aisles and Chad's eyes never wandered. The faster Doug would push the cart, the more Chad would smile. The trust was overwhelming.

That was twelve years ago. Now Chad was fourteen.

Jesus, Doug thought, *where did the time go?* The years moved so fast now. He looked back at Chad following him into the market. Chad was sullen. He had been such a happy kid growing up. But he was a quiet kid now. Doug was not sure if it was that Chad was going through high school or if it was the divorce. *Probably both,* he thought. It was a tough time for a kid. Chad was not an especially good looking kid, and he was starting to get acne, just like Doug did at that age. That's all a kid needed for his self-esteem.

"Do you want anything particular for the trip?" Doug asked.

"Whatever." Chad replied nonchalantly.

"How about some marshmallows, we could make some s'mores?"

"Whatever Dad."

This was the toughest part of a divorce. Doug got angry at Chad for having a bad attitude, but he couldn't punish him or scold him. He didn't feel empowered. He felt he had to raise his tolerance levels, higher than before the divorce. Doug was not a power hungry guy but not having the same authority that he once had with his own child was difficult to bear. Especially when he thought that discipline would be better for the kid.

"Well, how about I get some and you can decide later if you want to roast marshmallows?"

"Sure Dad," the same monotone response.

Doug rolled the cart down the aisles as Chad followed a distance behind, far enough that Doug could not start a conversation with him. Fun trip so far. Doug went through his list of things to get: water, ice, eggs, bacon, juice, macaroni and cheese, sandwich meat, and beer.

As Doug was turning a corner, he looked back to see where Chad was, but he didn't see him in the aisle. He waited a little bit, but no sign of his son. Maybe Chad had blown him off. The market was only about a mile from the house. Chad could have just walked out of the market and gone home.

Doug felt embarrassed. He waited a little bit more. Chad was not coming. He wasn't going to go on the trip by himself. The whole point was to do something with his son. If Chad went home, there was no way he would go back to the house and get him again. Doug started to think about what he had said to him. *Was suggesting s'mores at the campfire too childish?* he questioned. Chad wouldn't get upset enough to walk home if he had said something stupid. Or maybe he would? Doug didn't spend enough time with him to know. Not sure what to do, he turned the corner of the aisle and headed down the next one.

Chad was standing right there. "What?" Chad asked, seeing the look on his dad's face. He had some film rolls in his hands. He had gone back to another aisle to get some film for his camera. He approached Doug and dropped the film in the basket. The look of relief on Doug's face seemed to bring a spark to Chad's demeanor.

Doug felt a lot better, surviving a minor crisis. "You like to take pictures?"

"Sometimes." Chad said as they started moving down the aisle again.

"You interested in photography?" Doug asked.

"That would stand to reason, if I like to take pictures." Chad killed the chance at a good conversation.

They filled the basket full of the items on Doug's list, paid the cashier and made their way out to the SUV. Doug pulled the food out of the bags and packed the cooler, finishing up by placing a layer of ice bags on top of the food and shutting the lid. Chad, all the while, stayed in the front seat and loaded film into his camera. Doug closed the back door to the SUV, got into the driver's seat and without a word, drove off.

Doug continued to try to initiate conversations with his son, but Chad was not very talkative. Doug felt more comfortable now that they were driving. At least Chad couldn't walk away from him while they were in a moving car. Doug handed a map to Chad that Evan had made for them. It was actually one of those US

Geological Survey topographic maps with a trail to the campsite written in pen ink over the map. Doug could see the trailhead marked on the map. The path led northward up Highway 21 and then took a left off of the highway. The trail then proceeded past the road into an unmarked area and then stopped at an "X" marked with the word "camp".

"Uh, Dad, where are we going?" Chad asked in confusion.

"To a little campsite that only Evan knows about, up in the No Return."

"How's Evan?" Chad asked.

"Good. He wanted to tell you hello."

After a moment of silence, Chad stated, "I saw the gun in the back."

"Yup."

"Are we gonna do some hunting?" Chad asked.

"Maybe." Doug teased. *Great,* he thought, *he's interested.*

Chad paused for a moment and put the map down. With a perplexed look on his face, he asked, "Is that legal?"

Doug didn't have an immediate answer. He hadn't

even thought about it until now. And for Chad to even have the asked the question meant that he probably knew the answer. Of course it was illegal. The No Return was a National Forest. National Forests and Parks were wildlife refuges, not hunting grounds. What better way to spend a father-son weekend than doing something illegal together? Doug thought of trying to find a different place to go, where hunting was legal, but he didn't have a clue as to where. Any place that had game--that was not a National Park? Is that how it worked? He felt stupid.

"We don't have to hunt, we could just camp there?" Doug offered. He didn't like the fact that he was already compromising on the trip and they hadn't even gotten there yet. This was supposed to be his well thought out plan.

Chad looked at Doug. "Well, if Evan hunts there, it's probably fine."

Chad had offered the out and Doug took it, but he didn't like the reference to Evan. Even though Evan was his friend, Doug felt Chad liked Evan more than himself. It was selfish, but he wanted his son to like him the most. "Good." was all he could return.

With Evan's map, Chad gave directions to the campsite. They got off the 21, and headed due north onto a dirt road, straight into the No Return Wilderness. Due to the remoteness, there were few road signs, but they could tell clearly enough where they were as the wilderness crept in around them. The smoothly packed dirt road meandered for a few miles, until it led to a bumpier road, covered with loose rocks. Another twenty minutes of driving then lead to a fire access road off to the right. Although the directions were fairly easy to follow, it was slow going. The fire road showed little signs of maintenance. The trees and tall brush snapped against the windshield as the SUV trudged along. Doug was worried that the fire road would eventually just narrow and then end. But why would it just end? What would make a fire road end?

The road became more uneven. The SUV stumbled over an old log that was camouflaged by the underbrush. The vehicle hit it hard, lurched over the barricade and slammed to the ground on the other side. As the second axle cleared, the SUV came down even harder and the momentum made Chad hit his head on the ceiling.

"Ow, fuck!" Chad spurted as he quickly rubbed his head.

"Sorry Chad. You OK?" Doug asked with his eyes still focused on the road.

"Yeah, I'll live." Chad replied, wincing from the pain.

Doug looked over, wondering why he hadn't hit his head, even though Chad had. He realized that Chad was not wearing his seatbelt.

"Put your seatbelt on." Doug commanded.

"I said I'm fine." Chad shot back.

"I didn't ask if you were fine. I said put your seatbelt on." Doug was going to ask if Ellen let him sit in the car without wearing one, but he thought better of it. Doug slowed down the SUV to a stop, waiting for Chad to respond.

"OK, OK, it's going on!" Chad clipped the shoulder strap into the buckle. Doug responded by driving forward. Another mile or so rolled by, and they came to a fork in the fire road.

"Take a left." Chad stated looking at the map.

"You sure?"

"Not really. Evan drew in an offshoot from the main path. That must mean that this road goes off to the right, but we stay left." Chad reasoned.

"God, how did Evan find this place?" Doug was perplexed.

They arrived an hour later at Evan's campsite, designated by a Budweiser can nailed into the trunk of a tree. *Very Evan,* Doug thought, *Camp Intoxicated.* He pulled the vehicle into the clearing, and pulled a u-turn so that they could unload the camping gear easier. Chad helped Doug with the tent. It was one of those older, triangular shaped tents. It looked like it hadn't been used in twenty years. Doug guessed that

Evan must have slept in the flat bed of his truck when he came out here. With a little help from a tree and a lot of rope, they managed to get the thing upright.

"You want to start the fire while I get the food hoisted into the tree?"

"Sure, are we rushing for any particular reason?" Chad asked.

"Well yeah, I wanted to get in a little hunting before nightfall. What do you think?"

"Sounds fine, Dad." Chad said things in such a tone that Doug couldn't tell if he was being sarcastic or not. It was frustrating for Doug, but he had decided not to push it. Let Chad be a wise-ass for a little while. Maybe it was his God given right as the son of a divorced Dad.

Chad gathered a healthy collection of dry wood from the immediate area. It wasn't hard to find, because the place hadn't been picked apart like an official campsite. The only person that camped here was Evan. Chad got the campfire going with kindling and then threw in the larger logs. All the while Doug was hoisting the cooler into the Ponderosa tree, with a large branch hanging over the campsite.

"Nice campfire." Doug commended.

"Thanks, should we be leaving it?" Chad asked, obviously feeling concerned.

Doug thought about it for a moment. Sure, the fire could spread, but there was no wind and the fire was a good fifteen feet from the nearest brush. "It'll be fine," he concluded.

Doug pulled the shotgun and ammunition from the SUV, along with a six-pack of beer. He then walked across the camp to a trail on the other side that went deeper into the woods. Chad followed.

It was a narrow trail, wide enough for one person. The path wound through the dense trees which blocked most of the sunlight, except for the occasional ray peeking through the canopy of firs. *What a neat place,* Doug thought. It had a foreboding feel. The woods seemed old, like it had been this way for a long time and wasn't going anywhere. It was not like the growth that immediately surrounded the town of Omah, which was mostly comprised of young trees and saplings. The trees here were tall and wide-reaching, creating a blanket for the under-forest. The shadows were dense and plentiful. Sunlight was the exception to shadow.

About a quarter of a mile from camp, they spotted the makeshift blind that Evan had made the last time he was there. It was just a wall of sticks with some soft ground behind it to sit on. Beyond the blind was a decent view of a clearing of tall grass with a dense wall of forest behind it. The two of them sat down while Doug loaded the gun, following the steps that Evan had instructed him on. He put four shells into the magazine chamber.

"I didn't know you knew how to use a gun." Chad said.

"To be honest, I didn't know until this morning."

"Great. I feel safe." Chad pretended to sound worried.

After about a half hour of nothing, Doug cracked open a beer and handed it to Chad, and then opened another one for himself. He figured that Chad could have a beer by now. Better that Chad have his first beer in front of him while he knew that they would be camping overnight together, rather than out with some friends off the road somewhere with a car to crash. Chad quietly welcomed the beer.

"You got a girlfriend yet?" Doug always asked the same question.

"No Dad. Not yet." Chad shrugged.

"Well you should, you're a good-looking kid. Take after your Dad in that department." It was the same bad routine, but for some reason it made Chad relax.

Chad gulped at the beer. "This stuff tastes like shit. How can you stand it?"

Doug was a little taken aback by Chad's mouth. He was tempted to discipline him, but once again he felt powerless. He decided to let it go. "You get used to the taste of beer, son. It tasted pretty bad when I first tried it."

"I'm not saying beer tastes bad, just this crap that you buy. What was it, four bucks a case?"

Doug laughed. Chad had apparently drunk beer before. That parental responsibility rush came over Doug, but again, he decided to let it slide. Chad was going to drink alcohol sometime, and it was rather pointless to get mad at him for it after he had just offered him a beer. Doug wished that he was around Chad more. His son was getting to that age when Doug could start to treat him as an equal.

"Well, actually, it was *five* bucks for the case. But shut up." Doug crushed the empty beer can and threw it at Chad. "Consider it free because you didn't pay for any of it!" Chad laughed, dodging the beer by rolling onto his back.

Out of the corner of his eye, Chad noticed a large animal moving slowly in the field in front of them, about one hundred feet away. It was big and had dark fur. Chad lifted himself off of the ground, and straightened himself to get a better look. Chad whispered, *"Dad, it's a bear!"*

Doug stood up into a semi-crouched position to peek his head over the blind. Excited, he lifted his rifle and rested it on the top of the blind. He targeted the animal in the gun sight. All he could see in the tall grass was a dark shape. The only two things he could determine was that it was furry, so it could not be a person, and dark enough that it was probably a black bear. It didn't look big enough to be a grizzly. Evan warned him about bears but he hadn't said anything about hunting them. What if the gun he had was not powerful enough? He didn't want the thing to charge them if he missed. He hesitated.

Chad urged, "Shoot it, Dad!"

That was all that Doug needed to hear. The gun fired with a loud crack, the stock of the weapon recoiling into his shoulder. Doug's eyes closed in reaction but he immediately opened them to see what had happened. He had hit the animal. It spun awkwardly, its human-like arm flinging around, and it let out a strange cry as it landed on its back. It was a strange motion, very unexpected for a bear.

Doug and Chad exchanged worried glances as they moved from behind the blind towards the animal. They walked through the tall grass hesitantly. As they got closer, they could see the dark shape lying on its back. Doug's stomach dropped as he saw the shape, a human form, sprawled out on the ground. The one thing that Doug was really worried about when he decided to take Chad hunting was that he might shoot some other hunter out here. And to see the man-like body lying on the ground made his heart skip a few beats. But something was very strange about the lifeless human form. It was covered in fur from head to toe. His fears turned to wonder as he realized what he had shot. It was not human, but it was not an animal either.

It was a Bigfoot.

"Holy shit, Dad! Is that what I think it is?"

It was a moment of adrenaline, repulsion, curiosity and awe. The creature looked to be about six feet tall with dark skin, covered in short black-brownish fur. A bloody hole was evident on the left chest, from where the shotgun blast had exited the body. Blood was pumping out of the hole and spreading across the chest and dripping onto the dry grass.

Doug and Chad jumped back as the creature jerked from some kind of spasm. The thing turned its head towards Doug. Its eyes were large, round and almost completely black, aside from the reflection of the setting sky. Doug could hear the breathing of the animal now. Its raspy intake was emanating from the wide mouth. The creature lay on its back, palms open to the sky, as if in a pose of questioning. The labored breathing slowed even further. It then took in one long gasp. The black eyes were locked on Doug's. That was the last breath. The creature died with its eyes open. Its expression of disbelief permanently held in place as its life force slipped away.

Doug's first kill as a hunter was an animal that no one thought even existed. It was a confusing moment. He couldn't tell if the adrenaline that poured through him was from the first-time kill or from the fact that this was an animal that no one believed was real. He was not sure how the future would play out, but he knew that today had taken on life changing ramifications.

Chad was excited. "Are we going to be famous?!"

"I, uhh, probably." Doug acknowledged, caught up in the excitement.

Chad started running back towards camp, remembering that he had left his camera in the SUV.

"I'll be right back!" Chad exclaimed with excitement.

Doug took a closer look at the creature. It was startling how human the thing looked. The creature had three-inch hairs covering its entire body except on the face, palms and bottom of its feet. It was definitely more like hair than fur. It was almost matted, with longer hair going down the back of the neck and arms. Its feet and hands were very similar to a human's, five fingers and toes. The fingers were thick and short with an extended palm. Its face was strong looking, like a primitive man. The nose was broad and upturned with large flared nostrils. The humanoid had a large protruding brow, a straight line going across the forehead. The cheeks were large and high. The top of the head was slightly pointed, similar to a male silverback gorilla. It had strange smell, like really bad body odor.

But there was something odd about the creature. It was not exactly how he would have pictured a Bigfoot to look. Its skin seemed smooth, almost youthful, and judging by how those 70's documentaries described them, these things were bigger than eight feet tall.

This animal looked no taller than six feet. It looked skinny, like a gangly teenager.

He had shot a young one.

At that moment, the most powerful, blood-curdling roar blasted through the woods. The sound nearly knocked Doug off of his feet. As he wheeled around to determine its origin, a sickening feeling started to bubble in his stomach. The roar came from the direction of camp.

Chad!

Doug instantly started sprinting back towards camp, as fast as his legs could go. In the excitement he forgot the shotgun, still lying by the dead Bigfoot. He suddenly realized how much darker it had gotten in the past few minutes, for the woods had become black as he pushed through them. He ran as fast as he could, screaming for his son.

The creature roared again.

Chad was at the edge of camp and the darkness had already set in. He knew something or someone was very close to him, but he couldn't see anything. The glow of the campfire was up ahead. The woods around him were deadly silent. He wanted to be home. He decided to make for the SUV, lock the doors and wait for his dad. The snap of a twig came from directly behind him. Chad stopped moving. A huge shadow reared up as he turned around whimpering, *"Dad?"*

His answer came in a low growl.

CHAPTER THREE

The branches whipped into Doug's face as he ran through the forest. He tried to stay on the trail as best he could, but it was hard in the waning light. He heard his son's screams through the trees. They sounded horrible. The screams were not cries for help. They were cries of pain. Chad was clearly being attacked. Doug ran on.

Suddenly, Chad's screaming stopped. Doug yelled for his son, imagining the worst. He sprinted past exhaustion, leaping over logs and fallen branches, making his way through the darkened woods. The short hike from the blind seemed close before, but so distant now. If only Chad had stayed with him. He could only imagine what an adult Bigfoot looked like. His fears barraged him with dark visions, aided by the look of what he had shot. The young one probably had the strength to kill him. What kind of power did an adult have? Only then did he realize that he had forgotten Evan's shotgun. He could not stop and turn back. There was no time. Chad did not have the time. Doug's fears told him that he may already be too late.

Doug burst through the trees and made it to the camp. He scanned the campground. There Chad was, lying oddly on the ground, facedown, near the campfire. Doug ran to the boy, gently flipped him over, and cradled him in his arms. Chad was lifeless, but still warm to the touch.

"Chad, wake up!" Doug pleaded, "Please Chad."

The boy did not respond. There was no sign of blood, but Chad was covered in dirt. Doug found it horrifying to imagine that something powerful had attacked his son to the point of rendering the boy unconscious. He picked up Chad's limp body and stood up.

Just then, from where Doug had emerged from the woods, was a massive dark figure. Doug was only alerted to the creature's presence by its breathing, but it was unmistakable what the thing was. The Bigfoot took a powerful step out of the trees into the campsite. *Holy God.* It was huge. Doug backed away from it with Chad in his arms, toward the center of camp. He made his way closer to the SUV.

Now the campfire was between him and the creature, and the fire's glow faintly illuminated the giant humanoid. The hair raised on the back of Doug's neck, an involuntary reaction, as his mind registered just how big the creature truly was. It was at least ten feet tall and wide, impossibly wide. Large round shoulders the size of basketballs with long powerful arms hanging down below the knees. Hair covered its entire body except for the face. The face itself was terribly menacing. It had a huge protruding brow setting the eyes almost completely in shadow, were it not for the campfire casting bright orange glints in the creature's eyes. Its face resembled something between a Neanderthal and a gorilla. Doug backpedaled his way to the car, putting distance between himself and the creature. The Bigfoot then crouched down into a striking position and roared once more. Doug simply could not believe what he was seeing.

He turned and made a run for the car, with the lifeless Chad in his arms. Not looking back, Doug carefully slung Chad over his right shoulder, freeing his left hand to grab the keys from his pocket and open the driver door. At a calm moment it would have been a dexterous challenge, but under the current conditions it was nearly impossible. He had to concentrate or they would both be dead. The larger car key materialized out of the jumble of metal in his keychain. He switched his grip and jammed the key into the lock, turning it twice to unlock all of the doors. On the window of the SUV side door, he could see the firelight become eclipsed by a huge shadow. It was coming. He dared not turn around to see. He hurriedly opened the backseat door, and rolled Chad off of his shoulder and placed him in the backseat. Thunderous footsteps came closer to the vehicle. Doug jumped into the driver's seat as the creature slammed into the back of the SUV. The thing must have covered ninety feet in four seconds. Doug floored it as the creature started to make its way to the driver's door. A huge black-skinned hand smashed the window as the SUV pulled away and headed off down the fire road into the night.

Doug, with a completely unconscious Chad rolling around in the backseat, drove like a madman down the fire road. He was somewhat lost. The road merged with another fire road from the left, but it didn't jog his memory. He stayed right rather than making the sharp turn to the left. *Thank God there are not too many options on these back roads,* he thought. He looked back at Chad, seeing no movement at all. The SUV rocked up and down as it sped down the fire road at thirty miles per hour. Doug took one hand off the wheel to steady Chad from falling into the floor gap in front of the backseat. The SUV was moving so fast through the dense alleyway of vegetation that Doug had no chance to respond safely to the road. The vehicle careened down the path, knocking away small saplings and underbrush. It was impossible to avoid all of the encroaching trees, so Doug stayed focused on dodging the larger ones, letting the smaller vegetation plow into the front of the vehicle. But his luck could not, and did not last. The vehicle lurched as it smashed into a large log, becoming stuck in the barricade. Doug jammed the accelerator, hoping to ride over the mass of wood, but the axle could not clear the main log. He shifted into reverse and backed up twenty feet. *It must have been the same log that Chad had hit his head on,* he thought. There was a much larger ditch on this side of the barricade, which made it tougher to surmount. What could he do? The embankment on either side looked too steep to drive over. He thought he could possibly clear the mass of trees with his bare hands, but how long would that take? Abandoning the vehicle and setting out on foot was not an option either. It was too far to carry Chad out of these woods.

Doug glanced in the rear view mirror. The whole view moved. Something close was moving from behind the SUV towards him. Something huge. He involuntarily screamed and floored the gas. He spun the wheel to the right, clearing the barricade and riding up the embankment at a dangerous angle. The four-wheel drive kicked in as all four wheels dug into the ground. Dirt and leaves ejected from the rear tires as Doug frantically tried to maintain traction and balance of the vehicle. He aimed the vehicle at an upward angle so that it would not tip. Chad was jostled around in the backseat, but Doug was too occupied to react. He had to focus on driving, for if the SUV tipped, it would have been all over. No one was within twenty miles of them. Doug could feel the balance of the SUV dangerously shift towards the driver's side. Once he cleared the barricade, he sharply turned the wheel back towards the fire road, angling the vehicle at a sharp downward decline. Once on the road, he then righted the vehicle and accelerated down the access way.

Doug did not look back.

He had only stopped at the barricade for a few moments, and the creature had caught up to him. He had no idea how far he had traveled from camp or how long it had taken to get to this point. He was disoriented, but he had to get Chad out of there. He could not make a mistake now and had to stay focused and keep the vehicle moving. He could not remember if there were any more large logs up ahead. The dim beacon of the headlights only revealed what lie twenty yards beyond the SUV, and with the overgrowth, most of it was cast in stark shadows. More trees came up ahead. The shadows created strange dancing shapes as the SUV rumbled over the uneven earth, an infinite tunnel of branches reaching out for him. The branches screeched along the sides as he passed them. Doug was starting to lose control. He had never been in a situation like this before. He felt like he was having a bad dream. The fire road continued on with no end in sight. His sweaty hands were now shaking which made it even more difficult to maintain control of the wheel.

A break in the trees finally appeared. The fire road gave way to the wider dirt road. His mind was so scrambled that he couldn't remember which way he had come from, just three hours earlier. Doug had lost sense of time and direction. The darkness did not help either, for there was no visual indication of which was the right way. His eyes finally went to the rear view mirror. Only a tunnel of trees appeared in the crimson hue of the brake lights. The creature was out there, somewhere. If he waited long enough, it would come for him. He turned left onto the dirt road and increased speed with the new terrain.

The road was still bumpy but seemed like a paved

highway compared to the previous road. He looked back at Chad, lying facedown on the backseat, the side of his face pressed against the leather cushion. Doug turned around and drove on, accelerating up to fifty miles per hour. If the road did not stop at a paved intersection, sooner or later he would have to make a decision to turn around. He could have been driving deeper into the No Return for all he knew.

The SUV barreled down the dirt road, kicking up a large trail of dust into the air. Doug's rear vision was completely obscured, but it didn't matter anymore. He had no need to look back.

Before long, he saw a paved road appear ahead at a T-junction. It must have been the Highway 21. He pulled onto it immediately, took a left, and floored it. Amidst all of the confusion, Doug had finally lost his bearings, and had turned in the wrong direction, away from the town of Omah. He accelerated to the top speed his SUV could go and sped down the two-lane highway.

Coming the other way, in an unmarked car was the Omah town sheriff, Darrell Williams, a full-blooded Salish Indian. He had been the sheriff of Omah for three months, coming from the reservation in Montana. Darrell had worked as the deputy sheriff on the Salish Indian Reservation for five years. His supervisor, another full-blood, was a good man to work for, but he wasn't leaving his post anytime soon.

Darrell felt that if he wanted to be a sheriff, he was going to have to relocate. Omah popped up as an option because it wasn't a sought out position. The pace was very slow, since there was barely any crime in Omah, mostly drunken disorderlies and domestic disturbances. It was appealing to Darrell because it would give him a chance to get his feet wet while not being overburdened. Darrell took the job, leaving very little behind. He was not married, and his only immediate family that was left was his mother. Omah had another good aspect in that it was not far from the Salish Indian Reservation, less than a day's ride.

He was driving in the opposite lane, heading back to town, when he saw Doug's SUV fire past him, well past the recognized speed limit. Darrell pulled a u-turn, put his red police light on the dashboard and followed Doug in pursuit. He reached almost 100 miles per hour before he started gaining ground on the SUV. Eventually, the unmarked car caught up to the vehicle.

Doug finally noticed that he was being pursued. He pulled his SUV over to the side of the road. Darrell pulled up behind him. Doug, not thinking rationally, immediately jumped out of his vehicle and headed towards the cop car. With a trained reaction, Darrell popped his door open, pulled out his gun, and aimed it through the open window. Doug screamed, "Help me! You gotta help me!"

"Don't move any closer! Stay cool buddy. Stay right where you are!" Darrell commanded.

Doug stopped moving towards the police car, but was still panicked. "I need help!"

"Just relax, put your hands up and tell me what's the matter," Darrell responded.

"My son was attacked! By this...animal."

"Where is your son?" Darrell questioned.

"He's in the backseat."

Doug backpedaled, gaining some composure, and Darrell followed him towards the backseat of the SUV, with his firearm still poised. He could see an adolescent boy in the backseat, facedown and motionless.

"Is he bleeding?" Darrell asked, concerned that the boy might need immediate medical attention. Darrell, like all officers, had a checklist of responses for traumatic medical situations.

"Not when I checked, but he's hurt bad. We have to get him to the hospital." Doug pleaded.

Darrell nodded, (observing that he was going the wrong way if he was going to the hospital, or back to town for that matter). Darrell was also intrigued at how the man could know that the boy was badly hurt, even though the boy was not bleeding. Darrell had a few more questions, but he decided not to ask the man until he got them to the hospital. "OK, I'll give you an escort back to Omah. Follow me."

The police car led the SUV down the main road towards the town of Omah. Along the way, the sheriff observed that the panicked driver was not always staying in his lane. He wondered if it was a good idea to escort the guy, rather than having everybody in his car, especially if the kid was really hurt. *It's these kinds of sudden situations that you have to be careful with.* Darrell thought. *Quick decisions have to be made, but they cannot be rash decisions.* Darrell had initially wondered if the driver had been drinking, but had dismissed the thought, considering the emergency situation.

Without incident, the two vehicles arrived at Omah's small municipal hospital. The emergency workers gently pulled Chad out of the SUV, laid him on a stretcher and pushed him into the hospital, with the two men in tow. The doctor began asking questions about what had happened to Chad, while checking for vital signs.

"What kind of animal was it?"

"Uh...I don't know," Doug stammered.

"Did you see it? Was it big?" the doctor asked, while checking Chad's pulse.

"Yes...I mean...I'm not sure." Doug stammered again.

The doctor seemed puzzled, finally making eye contact with Darrell, and he paused for a moment, "I guess it doesn't really matter, but if you remember anything, tell the nurse."

A nurse stepped up and blocked Doug from following them into the emergency room. "You'll have to wait out here, sir," she said firmly, gesturing to the waiting room. She handed Doug a clipboard. "Fill this out. The doctor will let you know as soon as he knows anything." She closed the door in front of him.

Darrell followed Doug over to the couches in the waiting room. Doug sat there looking despondent. The pen was shaking in his hand, hovering over the first line of the form, which asked for the patient's name.

"What is your son's name?" the sheriff asked.

"Chad." Doug whispered with his eyes closed.

"What's your name?"

"Doug Childress," he responded. He had dropped the pen, which now dangled from the string attached to the clipboard. His free hand went to his face and covered his eyes and rubbed his temples at the same time.

"Does Chad have any other family?" the sheriff asked.

"What?" Doug asked, lifting his head up and away

from his hand and opening his eyes. Darrell could see that Doug's mind was in a daze.

"Where is Chad's mom?" the sheriff rephrased his question.

"Uh, she's here in town." Doug responded.

"Maybe we should call her?" Darrell suggested. Darrell saw Doug's expression of disinterest.

Doug took in a deep breath, and paused. "Her number is 555-2539."

By Doug's response, Darrell determined that they were not living together, and that they were probably divorced. "I'll call her." The sheriff stated.

Ellen awoke to the phone. Instantly, she knew that something was wrong by the time of the call. She grabbed the phone off of the nightstand. "Hello," she said hesitantly.

"Hello, is this Ellen Loncar?" an unfamiliar voice asked.

"Speaking."

"Ellen, this is Darrell Williams of the Omah Sheriff's Department."

"Shit, what happened?"

"Ma'am, there's been an accident. Your son has been attacked by an animal."

"Oh my God."

There was an awkward silence. Darrell was never really good at bearing bad news, but who was?

"Your son is at the Omah Municipal Hospital..." By the time that Darrell was ready to explain Chad's condition, Ellen had already hung up the phone.

Pete Travers

CHAPTER FOUR

After a half hour of sitting in the waiting room, Doug looked out through the window to see Ellen's car drive into the hospital parking lot. Darrell brought her in to see Chad, along the way passing by Doug who did not move to acknowledge her. Ellen gave a very upset and confused look towards Doug.

Entering the emergency room, Ellen saw Chad's lifeless body on the table, and her hands went to her face in horror. Chad had a number of tubes entering his body as he lay under the bright inspection lights. The doctor acknowledged her as he was interpreting the readouts from the vital signs monitor.

"My baby," Ellen whimpered.

"Are you Mrs. Childress?" the doctor questioned.

"Yes..." she hesitated. "I'm Ellen Loncar. That's my son. What happened to him?"

"Is your son allergic to any kind of medications that you know of." The doctor asked as he scanned the boy's eyes with a pen-shaped flashlight.

"No." Tears started welling up in her eyes.

"Does he have any chronic medical conditions that we should know about – such as epilepsy or diabetes?"

"No."

"Thank you, Mrs. Loncar. And I'm sorry, but you will have to wait in the other room. We need to run some more tests." He urged her to leave the room.

"What kind of tests? What's wrong with him?" She cried.

"He's stable, but we are not sure yet what's wrong with him. He's been attacked."

"Attacked by what?"

"We're not sure. As soon as we know something, we will let you know." The doctor gestured towards the sheriff.

Darrell moved forward and escorted her back into the waiting room. Ellen saw a downtrodden Doug and anger welled up inside her.

"Where the hell did you take him?!" she screamed at

Doug. Still dazed, Doug was at a loss and could not respond.

The sheriff quickly determined that these two should not be in the same room. He persuaded Ellen outside to get some air and to put some distance between her and her ex-husband.

Doug could do nothing but wait. Darrell stayed outside with Ellen and consoled her, as best he could.

A little while later, the doctor walked earnestly out of the emergency room, obviously looking for somebody. Doug got up and the doctor deftly moved to the side, giving him a very concerned look and walked outside to get the sheriff. The doctor beckoned the sheriff, and they both went back into the emergency room, leaving Doug behind. Once they were within the confines of the room, the doctor spoke.

"Now, he said that an animal attacked the boy, right?" the doctor asked in a suspicious tone.

"Yeah, why?" Darrell asked, growing curious.

"Let me show you something," the doctor gestured towards Chad.

Chad was lying on his back on the table. He looked very cold. The doctor carefully rolled Chad up over onto his side. "Well, first of all, I can't find as much as a claw mark on the kid, and second of all, you see the bruises here? You see the shape?" Darrell could see four parallel bruise lines with large round shapes at the top. It was clear that it was a fist impression.

The doctor stated the obvious. "Animals don't punch."

Darrell's mind was already clicking. As the doctor was suggesting what might have happened, Darrell was on his CB radio, calling the sheriff's office for his deputy, Howard Forsythe. Darrell told the deputy to do a cross check on Doug Childress, and then to come down to the hospital. *This is going to get ugly,* he thought.

Deputy Forsythe arrived quickly and headed into the hospital. He went right for the sheriff and urged him to talk in private.

"The guy is not completely clean," Forsythe explained.

"What do you mean by that?" Darrell asked.

"There's a record of a domestic violence situation with his wife."

"Not good," Darrell said, "Is it repeated or an isolated case?"

"It appears isolated, but who knows how many times it went unreported." Forsythe commented with indignation.

"Don't presume too much Forsythe. When did the report get filed?"

"About one year ago, right before their apparent divorce."

"Was the violence towards just the wife?" Darrell asked.

"Yes, at least that's the only victim that appears in the police file. Why?"

"His son is in the emergency room. He has been beaten up pretty bad. The doc just told me that the wounds were not inflicted by an animal, which is Childress's story."

Forsythe grew angry at this statement. "Scumbag," he muttered.

Doug was watching things move quickly around him. The cops were getting a little jumpy. No one was talking to him, but everyone was looking at him funny.

His wife.

The divorce.

It clicked.

Oh, shit.

Doug didn't know what to do. He stood up. Who's gonna believe him? *"Bigfoot attacked my son."* It sounded ridiculous. Doug had been there, seen the thing, and it still seemed unreal. The sheriff and the deputy approached him and asked him to come quietly. They led Doug to an empty room in the hospital. The sheriff began to interrogate him about the incident.

"It was an animal of some kind but ... I'm not sure what it was." Doug pleaded.

"How can you not know? Did you see it?" Darrell asked.

"Yes, well not really. Not good. It was big,... that's all I know." Doug tried not to lie, keeping his story as truthful as possible, but it was difficult to say anything useful.

"So you saw the animal, but you couldn't tell if it was a bear or a mountain lion, or something else?" Darrell prodded.

"I don't know. It was dark." Doug feared his story was not going to fly.

"Bullshit, you lying piece of shit!" Forsythe raised his voice as he moved aggressively towards Doug. Darrell quickly moved between the two men and placed a calm hand on Forsythe. Darrell paused, thinking that his deputy might have been playing bad cop to his good cop, but playacting would have been out of character for Forsythe. He was really pissed. Darrell urged Forsythe to step back and calm down.

"Have you been drinking Mr. Childress?" Darrell

changed the direction of the interrogation.

"No." he stated, but his dazed memory was returning back to him. "Yes, but I only had one beer." That was one thing he didn't have to lie about.

Doug's statements sounded weak and everybody knew it. There was something in Doug's words, however, that struck Darrell's curiosity. *Doug was hiding something more than the obvious*, Darrel thought. *What was he hiding?*

Upon the sheriff's order, Deputy Forsythe roughly handcuffed Doug and took him to the police car. On the way out, Doug walked past Ellen, and urged, "Say something!" as he was put into the car. Ellen was confused by the statement, but was still so angry with him that she just turned and walked back into the hospital.

The sheriff told the doctor that he would be back later and walked out to his car. The two police cars rolled out of the parking lot. They arrived at the Omah Police Station, about a ten-minute drive. It was a tiny place with one jail cell, into which they promptly put Doug.

"I am going to stop by the hospital in the morning before I check in. I am going to see how the boy is doing." What the sheriff didn't say was that he wanted to have a longer chat with Ellen, to find out more about Doug.

"Poor kid," Forsythe stated. "I am going to finish up

the paperwork, and then head upstairs."

"Thanks Forsythe. Good night." Darrell thanked him and left the station.

Doug was completely paralyzed with indecision. He had to do something. His son was in critical condition, and the police believed he was responsible. He felt like he was in the backseat of a car with no driver, and no brakes, accelerating down a hill. His explanation of what had happened was incomplete. Doug feared that the truth would make him sound either delusional or wildly deceptive, and he was certain that they had found his domestic violence record. His situation was looking grim. *Why did she do that to him?* She could've told the truth to the divorce court, and she would have gotten custody of Chad regardless. They never give custody of a child to the father over the mother. If only he had some kind of proof that it wasn't him who had injured Chad. But what did he have?

The body.

He had to show them the dead Bigfoot! If they saw the body, he could use it as an alibi for what had attacked Chad. It wasn't the same creature that had actually attacked his son, but that didn't matter. It was a Bigfoot, for God's sake! They would believe anything he said, once they saw the body. But how would he get them to see it? He thought of beckoning for the deputy, but reconsidered the situation. The truth was unbelievable. He felt there was no chance that he could convince the police to drive him back into the wilderness to look for a supposedly fictitious animal. And besides, he'd probably get lost trying to find his way along those fire roads. But Evan knew how to get there. He felt a twinge of hope. He asked to use the phone to make his one call.

Forsythe sat there and did not respond.

"I would like to have my one phone call, please." Doug repeated.

But Forsythe was not responding. He just sat at his desk, staring straight at Doug without blinking. There was a deadness in his eyes, a cold stare. Forsythe then picked up the phone and called the hospital. He got the doctor on the line, to go over the case. Forsythe repeated what the doctor was saying as he typed it into the report. He made sure that he spoke loud enough so that Doug could hear every word.

"...major contusions around the left arm and lower back. Fist impression on the upper middle back, under the shoulder blade. Bottom two ribs broken along with a fractured clavicle...deep coma...possible internal bleeding...Got it Doc." Forsythe looked at Doug as he finished the conversation with the doctor. It was the same unblinking stare.

Doug was a mixture of emotions. He was deeply saddened by what he had just heard about Chad's condition and frustrated that he could not help. "Look, I need to make a phone call. I have something very important to show you that proves my innocence..." Doug pleaded.

Forsythe cut him off. "You know, my dad abused me."

Doug backpedaled away from the jail bars.

"And you know what the worst thing about it was? It wasn't the fact that he would beat me up real good and I would be covered with bruises. No, that wasn't the worst of it. You know what it was?" Forsythe pulled out his gun and approached the cell. "It was all of the fucking excuses that he would make up as to why I was so fucked up." Forsythe took his revolver and slid it across the jail bars, casually pointing the barrel towards Doug. Doug had backed up all the way to the far side of the cell.

"Some kids are clumsy." Forsythe continued, imitating his father. "I had to fucking pretend that I kept tripping so that he could beat me up some more." Forsythe pointed the gun directly at Doug. "You know, I should kill you right now, but you know what, by the looks of it, you won't be beating your son anymore. And I think it'll be better if you stay alive for a long time, sit in the state prison and have nothing better to do but think about what you did to him." Forsythe pulled the gun away and walked away from the jail cell towards the front door. As deputy, Forsythe was given board in a room above the station. He headed outside to the stairs that lead up to the second floor.

Doug did not move away from the back wall of the jail

cell. Eventually, he slid down the wall until he was crouched on the cell floor. His head dropped as he cradled his knees towards his shaking body.

He raced through his options but all of the possibilities or courses of action dropped away as quickly as they entered his mind, all except one.

Doug had to figure out a way to get out of there on his own.

Pete Travers

CHAPTER FIVE

The jail cell was cold and dark. The lights were turned off, but there was still enough dim illumination from the exit signs above the doors to see around the station. Determination started building in Doug. He had to break out of the jail cell. From upstairs, he could hear Forsythe having a one-way conversation with somebody. Forsythe must have been on the phone. Doug could hear him laughing. After a half hour, the conversation stopped, followed by a long stretch of silence. Forsythe must have gone to bed.

Minutes turned into hours of thinking and looking around. A toilet and a foldout cot were the only contents in the sterile chamber. The walls and floor were painted concrete. A panel of thick steel bars with a locked gate comprised the remaining wall. Doug determined the only way out of the cell was with the key, which was, of course, nowhere in sight. *Where would you put the key to the cell?* The first logical place he could think of was the top drawer of the deputy's desk, which was about six feet away. Unfortunately, the wooden desk was facing away from him. Doug took off his belt and held it outside of the jail bars. He flung one end out in an attempt to pull something useful off of the desk. Eventually, he was able to knock a plastic mug off the desk, and it took a lucky bounce towards him. He kept dragging on it with his belt until it was within arm's reach. Doug stopped for a moment to listen if the noise he was making had alerted the deputy upstairs. After hearing nothing, he resumed. He then took one of his shoelaces and tied it between the belt buckle and the mug, making a makeshift bolo. Doug swung the bolo under the cell bars toward the legs of the desk. After many tries, he got the mug to make a sweeping arc and tie itself up nicely under the closest leg. With a steady hand, he pulled on the belt. The desk slid along the smooth concrete floor towards the cell. He managed to get the desk right to the edge of the jail bars, where he swung it around to get at the front drawers. Bingo! A chain with a half-dozen keys was inside.

Doug fumbled with the keys and tried to open the cell. His excitement waned as he tried each key and, one by one, they failed to open the lock. With the last key in hand, he jammed it into the lock and tried to turn it. Nothing. His hopes sank. The cell key must be somewhere else. His situation had become worse. There was no way to push the desk back to its original position. Its misplacement would reveal his intention to escape. He sat back on the jail cot with his hands covering his face. Several minutes passed before he

cleared his eyes and scanned the cell one more time.
Looking more closely at the lock, he recognized the
shape of the inset. Centered on the metal plate, were
the words "Taggamill Smithing Co." The logo seemed
very familiar. He remembered. It happened to be the
same logo as the one on the vault's lock at the bank.
It was a detail that he viewed several times a day
during the week, but had never paid attention to.
Thinking about it, he realized how similar the doors
were. He checked his shirt pocket. Through all the
turmoil, the bank key chain was still there. It was
amazing that he hadn't lost it somewhere in the
woods. Knowing it was a foolish notion to think that
the bank key would work, he tried it anyway.
Surprisingly, the key slid in smoothly. But when he
tried to turn it, the key wouldn't rotate. As he jimmied
it around, he could sense that it was a pretty close
match, as if there were minor differences between his
key and the real cell key.

Doug continued to aggressively try the lock with his
bank key, sliding it around. He didn't think it would
work right away, but he hoped that he could scrape
the key up enough, along its teeth, to determine where
on the key the discrepancies were. After a few minutes
of working the key, Doug pulled it out and examined
it. In the dim light, he could see that most of the
abrasions had occurred on the back side of one tooth.
Clearly, that's where the locking pins were different.
He had to figure out a way to get the tooth shaved
down. He went back to the drawer and looked for
some kind of a file. He didn't see anything useful until
he spotted a small black leather case holding a square

tool inside. It was a Leatherman, one of those all-in-one Swiss Army knife kind of tools. He flipped it open, and pulled out all of the accessories inside the main grips. Sure enough, one of the options was a file. He braced the key against his thigh and put all of his leverage into grinding away at the specific tooth with the Leatherman.

Minutes rolled by as he worked the key. He held it up to the light. He had made progress. Not much, but he definitely had bit into the tooth. It felt warm to the touch from the friction. He continued, even more aggressively, putting his shoulder into it. He got from his crouched position and tried the key again. It slipped through the locking mechanism now. He heard a loud click and the door swung open. *Wow, I did it. I'm free.*

Okay, next step, Doug thought, *I need a car.* He found the keys to the deputy's police car on the key chain from the desk drawer. Doug pondered the circumstances for a moment as he snuck out to the car. The gravity of his situation was getting worse every minute. *Well, if I wasn't in trouble before, I sure am now.* He thought about calling Evan now that he could use the phone. *No. It would only get Evan involved as an accomplice. Besides, Evan might not want to cooperate, considering that he would be breaking the law as well.* Doug decided to find his own way back to the campsite. It would take him longer, but he felt it was safer that way. Determination built again, as he realized this was his only chance to get out of his dilemma. He could and had to do this alone.

The police Crown Victoria started right up, and he quietly pulled out of the station and headed towards the campsite. By the time anyone was awake, he would be back with the body.

On the way out of town, he drove by the hospital. He wanted to stop and just stay with Chad. God, he hoped Chad was alive, but it didn't sound good. *Those assholes didn't even fuckin' bother to tell me if Chad was going to make it,* Doug thought angrily. From what he had overheard in Forsythe's phone conversation with the hospital, Chad had internal bleeding and was in a coma. Doug wanted so badly to go in there, but he knew that he would just get arrested again. He pulled the car over alongside the hospital curb. He had to get the Bigfoot body, then everything would be cleared up. Then he could sit by Chad when he woke up...if he woke up. *Jesus, why hadn't Ellen said anything?* She had hours already to let the cops know that he didn't abuse anybody. They were never going to believe him if she didn't say anything, unless he had the body. Doug could see Ellen's car in the hospital parking lot. She was still there. If she saw him, she would report him and he would be caught again, before he had time to clear himself. He pressed the accelerator and drove the car towards the edge of town.

Meanwhile, Ellen was sitting by Chad, watching him, waiting for him to wake up. She was completely confused about the whole night. She wondered what

Doug had meant by "Say something!" They hadn't asked her too many questions, and suddenly Doug was whisked off to jail. It didn't sit right. Doug was a jerk sometimes, but he would never have done this to Chad. She knew he worshipped their son.

What had happened? Ellen knew they were going camping, but she didn't know where. It didn't seem important at the time, because Doug would be there. He was a piece-of-shit husband, but a very reliable, very protective father. It seemed odd that he would have chosen camping as something to do for fun. It just wasn't like him.

Doug traveled down the highway towards the turnoff. The road became a soft haze ahead of him, the white and yellow lines of the two lane highway blurring across the stark contrast of the black asphalt. He hadn't pulled an all-nighter in years, not since Chad was a baby, and the lack of sleep was taking its toll. His eyelids were feeling heavier and heavier. He was drifting. A moment passed, and his head jerked back jolting him into consciousness. He looked out the windshield and could see he was still on the road. How long had he drifted off? Was it a second? Five seconds? He was not sure, but he was still in his lane. The flash of panic gave him a moment's respite from the lurking fatigue in his body.

The dirt road turnoff came and went. Doug registered the familiar markings of the passageway into the No

Return a full hundred yards after he had passed it. He
pulled a u-turn, doubled back, and angled right onto
the dirt road. He had to slow down to forty miles per
hour on the narrow road, and could feel the rocks hit
the underbelly of the Crown Victoria. He turned on
the brights, which illuminated the forest around him.
The shadows were dark and shifting. Shapes were
starting to emerge from the trees. Dark shapes. He
was returning back to a place he never wanted to be
again and was going in alone. He wished he had
contacted Evan. His friend was familiar with these
woods and would have probably calmed his fears, but
more importantly, Evan would have been able to help
carry the body.

Time passed as he sped down the dirt road. This time,
he recognized the fire road before he had passed it.
The Crown Victoria's powerful engine hummed as he
traveled down the crowded access way. A mile or so
down the road, he came to the log barricade. He
slowed the car to a stop in front of it.

The fear came on him in a rush. He remembered the
image in the rearview mirror. He remembered the
vision of the creature at the camp. He became aware
of the noise coming from the engine. It was too loud.
He was probably alerting every damn creature in the
whole woods to his presence. He looked out the side
window. He could not see more than five yards with
the dim red glow from the brake lights. The Bigfoot
could be standing right there, and he would not have
been able to see it. It could be moving towards him
right now. All that he had for protection was a thin

sheet of glass.

He floored the gas pedal. The car flew over the barricade and crashed down on the other side front first and the back following shortly thereafter. He checked the rearview mirror and could see nothing but trees and dust. He drove on, realizing that his fear had driven him to make even more noise, which is exactly what he didn't want to do.

It was bad enough driving the SUV down the fire roads, but navigating the police car through woods was a challenge, especially with the lower axle clearance. A few times, the middle ridge in the road scraped against the bottom of the car.

A tiny glint appeared before him in the headlights. It was the beer can marking Evan's camp.

He pulled the police car into the camp and turned off the ignition. As he opened the car door, the internal light came on and illuminated the interior of the vehicle. The flash of light blinded him to the darker woods around the car. He quickly closed the car door, shutting off the ceiling light. He waited to let his eyes adjust. He felt riddled with panic. *Was he too scared? No.* If anybody else had seen what he had seen, they would not have come out here alone. His eyes adjusted to the pre-dawn darkness. He could make out the faint shapes of the immediate woods around him. Nothing moved. He rolled down his driver's side window a few inches to listen. Faint sounds came in. A slight breeze was rustling the trees. A bird chirped in the distance. He sat motionless, pulling in the sounds of the forest. The front windshield should have shown the fire pit and the trail beyond which led to the blind. However, all he could see in that direction was blackness. It was the same direction that the creature had come from when Doug had found Chad lying on the ground. The earlier vision of the beast illuminated by the campfire dominated his consciousness. What would he do if it came at him right now? He had no defense. No weapon. Suddenly, he remembered that the shotgun was at the blind. He felt stupid and weak. He felt scared. Time was ticking away, but he could not bring himself to get out of the car. The darkness was overwhelming. The walk to the blind seemed too far to go without a weapon or sufficient light, and he had neither. He checked the glove compartment of the police car for either a handgun or a flashlight, but all he found were speeding ticket forms and maps. He sighed at the futility.

He checked his watch, which read 4:30am. When would the police discover he had broken out of jail? The vision before him did not change. Blackness. But dawn would be coming soon. The minutes dragged by as he fought the fatigue. He did not want to fall asleep for it would be costly if he woke up hours from now, but he could not move until he had some light. Time passed as he sat in his own stalemate. His hands went to the wheel. He wished he could just drive to the blind.

He heard something move ahead of him in the

campsite. It was close, not even ten yards ahead. His shaking hand went slowly to the headlight switch. In the hour he had been at the campsite, the light had slowly increased, enough to make out faint shapes. Something moved ahead. He thought about what he would do if it was the creature. The only thing he could think of was to use the car as a weapon. He would fire up the ignition and ram the thing. His fingers closed around the headlight knob. He popped on the car's headlights, illuminating the campsite.

He screamed involuntarily at the movement before him. Fifteen feet high, swinging like a pendulum, was Evan's cooler. A raccoon was balancing on top of it, trying to get inside, obviously smelling the food. The added weight of the raccoon, which must have climbed down the rope to get at it, had thrown the cooler out of balance. The raccoon just stopped and stared in the direction of the headlights, as it swayed back and forth. In the bright light, the raccoon's eyes glowed. It sat, frozen on its swinging perch. There was no fear in the animal, only curiosity.

The relief of the situation and the increasing light gave Doug enough courage to get out of the car. He moved across the campsite, walking under the raccoon and the cooler. The animal turned its head and looked over its shoulder as he passed behind it. He entered the woods by the dark trail. Without the protection of the car or a weapon, he felt extremely vulnerable. It was like walking a tightrope of fear. He either had to go back to the safety of the car, or strive ahead to the safety of the shotgun. It was just the in between part that was bad. The trail seemed longer than before.

Doug knew he was tired but he started jogging towards the blind. He tried to make his footfalls as quiet as possible. If the Bigfoot came at him now, he had no protection. He would not be able to outrun it, and he knew that there was no possible way that he would be able to defend himself.

Doug could see more light creeping through the canopy ahead. He was approaching the clearing. He got to the blind, and moved past it into the open space, walking through the tall grass towards where the body had fallen to the ground.

It was not there.

A depression was left in the grass where the body once was. Evan's rifle was still lying to the side. There was a spattering of blood on the ground. Doug's mind scrambled through the possibilities. There was no way that someone could have found the dead creature out here. Evan had told him that no one came this far out. Maybe animals ate it? *Nah, there's no way the thing could have been completely eaten, bones and all, in one night.* Maybe he did not really kill it? Maybe it walked away on its accord. *No way.* He had shot it right in the chest, and had watched the blood pump away until it was completely lifeless. Nothing could survive from a wound like that. Something must have taken it away. Looking at the surrounding grass, it didn't readily look like the dead body had been dragged away. A sickening feeling was building in his gut. He was getting a pretty good idea of what happened to the body, remembering the events from earlier in the night. He circled the perimeter until he found a deep depression in the grass about five feet away. It was a footprint. A huge one. He couldn't make out any details like toeprints, but he was sure it was in the shape of a giant footprint. It must have been from the adult Bigfoot that had attacked Chad. Five feet away another print appeared. They led off into the woods on the opposite side of the clearing. The situation seemed hopeless. How was he going to track this thing? Rage started to well up inside him. *All I needed was some evidence, and now I've got shit.* Why didn't it just leave the body here? What did the animal care? The young one was dead, so what's the point of moving it.

Doug had to think of the where the creature would have gone. *Use your head. Where would it go?* He paused to think. *It could go anywhere.* Doug was aware of the great size of the No Return. It happened to be largest expanse of untouched wilderness in the lower forty-eight states, and this thing had apparently marched off right into it. He had just broken out of jail, stolen a police car, and his alibi was that a creature, that no one really thinks exists, had attacked his son. Not good. It sounded like a bad tabloid headline: "Bigfoot Attacked My Son, But I Don't Have Any Proof!"

Doug grabbed the shotgun and started to move in the direction of the tracks. In the tall grass, it was fairly easy to track the creature, for the prints were made obvious by the flattened reeds. It was amazing how long its strides were, at least five feet of space between prints. He had to jump to match the gait of the giant sasquatch. Unfortunately, the tall grass didn't last forever, as the tracks lead into the forest. He remembered those stories of Indians who could track a man over any landscape in any weather. *How did they do that? What did they look for?* He came to the edge of the grass. Luckily, there was some underbrush beneath the canopy of Douglas firs. Without some kind of vegetation to pass through, he doubted that he would have been able to find tracks over hard ground. With the underbrush, he could look for broken branches and crushed leaves. Doug, with patience, found his way. He paid close attention to the breaks in the underbrush. The vegetation made the ground softer here too, so when some of the footprints showed up in the clear areas, he could make out their distinct shape. He put his workboot next to the best print he found. *Jesus Christ!* His boot looked so small as it sat completely inside the print with an inch to spare on each side.

He made his way for a couple of hours, feeling fortunate that the landscape hadn't changed much, and the prints, albeit a lot easier to follow in tall grass than this brush, were still trackable. One thing that he noticed was how deliberate the tracks were. The Bigfoot was not wandering at all. It seemed to be making a bee-line for something, or somewhere.

After a few hours of tracking, Doug realized he must have gone at least three miles into the wilderness. He looked back, and saw only woods. There was no distinguishing the direction from which he had just come, from the direction he was going. It was pure untouched wilderness. No trails or signs of human presence. People just didn't come here. Through the cracks in the forest canopy, he could see sky, and in the direction he was going, basically east, he could see a giant mountain range. It was the Sawtooth Mountains, a huge uninhabited range covered in ancient forests of Douglas firs and Ponderosa pine. Could a Bigfoot hide here? *Yeah, absolutely.* How could it not? Doug could walk in this direction for one hundred miles before he saw another sign of human civilization, and he was starting to think that he might have to do that. *Well, whatever it takes,* Doug thought. What was his alternative? Jail? He'd rather die out in these woods, especially if Chad was dead. *Chad.* He did not want to think about his son. It only brought him anguish.

Doug stopped for a moment and looked at his belongings. He had a shotgun with eleven shells, some not-so-warm clothes and nothing to eat. He was starting to think about hunger. He had brought a whole cooler of food with him for the weekend the night before, but that was back at the campsite. He figured it was too late to turn back. Doug felt that it was the story of his life. He was never thinking ahead. His life was a series of reactions, with very little planning. But there was no need to plan one's next meal when you lived inside civilization's walls. There's a fast food restaurant at every corner. Out here it was different. Lack of planning could result in your death.

Or Chad's death. Could he have prevented Chad's death? Doug was not sure. When Chad had run back to camp to get his camera, the thought had not even crossed Doug's mind that there was danger in the woods. It was obvious now, but back then, in the heat of the moment? He was not sure. The only thing he was sure of was that he would question his actions from last night for the rest of his life, for however long that lasted.

Doug started to look around for something edible. What can you eat in a forest? It's not like there are groves of orange trees out here. All he could see were trees and bushes. He couldn't even identify what kind of bushes they were. He couldn't tell a poisonous plant from an edible one. Feeling defeated, he decided he'd just keep tracking the animal and hopefully some berry bushes would show up or something. God, he felt ignorant. Is this even the season for berries? Was there a season for berries, or did they just grow all year round? He didn't even have a clue when things grew. Doesn't everything happen in the spring? Is that always the case? None of the answers he preciously needed were coming to him. Alright, keep moving, he thought. He didn't have to absolutely eat just yet, he just had to get the evidence. And when this was all done, he could go eat anywhere he wanted, but for now, he had to keep tracking the creature. Otherwise, he'd be eating prison food for a while.

Pete Travers

CHAPTER SIX

It was nine o'clock in the morning when Darrell showed up at the sheriff's office. He walked into the building to see Forsythe staring dumbfounded at the unoccupied jail cell.

"He escaped?!" asked Darrell.

"Yeah, and I'm not sure how. He managed to pull the desk over to the cell, but the keys weren't inside it. I had the keys on me last night when I went upstairs. The lock doesn't have any signs of a forced opening either. It's weird."

"That is strange. You sure there wasn't an extra set of keys in the drawer of the desk?"

"Uh, well, yes and no. I am absolutely certain that there was not a set of cell keys in the drawer. There was, however, a set of car keys. It looks like he stole my police car."

"Whoa." Darrell responded.

"Has this ever happened to you?" Forsythe asked.

"Uh, no. But I have never had to deal with a situation like this before." Darrell partially told the truth. He had dealt with domestic violence situations before. Unfortunately, they happened rather frequently on the reservation. An offender had never broken out of jail and stolen a police car, however. *This is odd,* Darrell thought. *If the guy had any brains at all, he'd dump the police car as soon as possible.*

"Forsythe, put out an APB on your car."

"Already done."

"Oh, good, ... have you heard anything?"

"Not a thing, he must have stashed it."

"Yeah, maybe." Darrell started to think. There was something odd about this whole thing. Childress was somewhat fitting the profile of a repeat offender, but Doug's demeanor seemed a little out of place. There was something about the way the guy responded to the charges. He seemed surprised, almost in shock at first. And there was no remorse or guilt when the charges came down on him. Childress seemed frustrated, like he wanted to say something but couldn't. What would the guy be hiding? He abused his wife, and now he abused his son. That should have been the end of the story, aside from the fact that Doug was missing. He was probably in Canada by now.

A manhunt made things a lot more complicated, with a lot more law enforcement entering the fray. Darrell did not look forward to that. A jailbreak was going to draw a lot of negative press as well.

The first thing Darrell wanted to do was to get more information. This whole thing seemed a little off and he wanted to get on the right track before they started setting up search parties.

"I am going to do some checking into things, Howard." Darrell contemplated for a moment. "I will communicate with you on the search party logistics once I find out where we are going to be looking."

"Got it chief, should we go with full weaponry?" Forsythe asked.

The sheriff had to think again. "Yeah, better safe than sorry."

The sheriff walked out the door as Forsythe got on the phone.

Darrell arrived at the hospital a short while later. He walked down the hallway to the nurse's reception area. Without a word, a sitting nurse regarded him and pointed to a room down the hall. He walked into the small room, its lone window facing the east. The morning sun basked the bed with light, casting a golden ambience over the sterilized surroundings. Ellen was there. Her chair was butted up against the railings along the bed, and she was leaning forward with her head resting on the bed, her arms folded under her chin. She was staring at her son.

Chad, although with a bit more color back into his skin, still looked completely comatose.

"Hello Ms. Loncar."

Ellen slowly turned towards him, as if waking out of a dream. "Sheriff," She acknowledged, slowly blinked, and turned her head back towards Chad.

Darrell continued the conversation, even though Ellen had no interest in talking to anyone. "Ms. Loncar, your ex-husband escaped from jail sometime last night and is at large. I was wondering if you had any idea of where he might have gone."

Ellen was surprised by the question and turned to face Darrell, "I don't have a clue where he might have gone. He broke out of jail? On his own?"

The sheriff could see the interest in Ellen's eyes. "Yes. Do you have any idea of who he might make contact with?"

That question seemed to have stung Ellen. "I have no

idea where he might have gone, nor do I care." Her statement was forced, as if she did not mean what she had just said.

Was Darrell reading her wrong or was there concern in her tone? That was rather unusual for the ex-spouse of an abuser. Spouses of abusers lived in fear for years and when they are finally released from the imprisonment of the relationship, there is typically very little room in the spouse's heart for the abuser.

"Look Ms. Loncar. I am not going to pry too much here. But I need you to tell me anything you might know that would help us find Doug. He's probably more of a danger to himself than anybody else right now, but we have to find him." Darrell looked straight into Ellen's eyes.

She was definitely guarded, but she didn't have the demeanor of a continually abused wife that protected her husband out of fear. This lady seemed really level, under the circumstances, but she seemed to be hiding something.

"Look, I honestly don't know anything. Talk to Evan, because I know they are close friends. He might know where he would be. But...I don't know."

"Evan who?"

"Evan Ratcliffe. He lives on the other side of town, past Old Town up on Creekbed Road. Doug and Chad went camping, so Doug probably got the idea from

Evan. Talk to him."

"I'll do that. Thanks." He didn't think he was going to get anything more out of her right now. Earlier, Darrell had left the station with the odd feeling that his suppositions from the night before might be incorrect. It was as if he was missing a piece of the puzzle, which made all of the other pieces seemingly disjointed. Now, Darrell left the hospital convinced that there was more to the story.

Darrell drove through Omah, past the practically deserted Old Town. As he turned onto Creekbed Road, signs of civilization drifted away and the density of homes became sparser. He arrived at the address of Evan Ratcliffe. Evan's place was a smaller home, a one-story house on a modest parcel of land. One could tell that Evan had put a lot of work into his house, obviously taking his trade home with him. What started as a typical tract home in Omah, now had vaulted gables, stone walls and bay windows. There was cut timber and numerous other materials lying around in front of the house, waiting to be used for future projects. It was clear that Evan treated his home as a perpetual project that would probably never exist in a complete state.

Darrell drove the car into the driveway and stepped out. Almost immediately, from behind a pile of stacked wood, came a bloodhound dog barking fiercely at the intruder. Darrell tried to appease the dog to get it to stop barking, but to no avail. And then the front door opened, with Evan coming out.

"T-Bone, quiet." stated Evan. The dog instantly stopped barking and sat at attention understanding that Darrell was not an intruder. The dog was well trained, and was now fully content to just watch the sheriff approach the house.

"Evan Ratcliffe?" the sheriff asked.

"Yes, that's me. How can I help you?" Evan responded in a casual tone. Darrell observed that Evan was not at all disturbed by the sheriff's presence. That led the sheriff to believe that Evan was unaware of the jailbreak.

"Hello Evan, I'm Darrell Williams, the Omah sheriff. Do you mind if I come in and ask you a few questions?"

"Sure..." Evan said as he gave Darrell a quizzical look.

The interior of the home had the same quality as the outside with vaulted ceilings and giant pine crossbeams. Darrell noted the hunting gear around Evan's place and the heads of animals including deer and elk mounted on the walls.

Evan walked into the kitchen and grabbed an already poured cup of coffee and leaned against the kitchen counter. "What can I do for you?"

"You know Doug Childress?"

"Yeah, he's a friend of mine."

"Are you aware of anything that happened last night?"

"No. What happened?" Evan asked.

"I pulled Doug over last night. He had Chad in the backseat, unconscious. Doug claimed that the boy had apparently been attacked by some animal." Darrell watched Evan's reaction carefully and noted that he seemed genuinely surprised.

"We brought Chad to the hospital, and the doctor suggested that it might not be an animal attack. We incarcerated Doug late last night, but sometime in the middle of the night, he broke out and stole a police car. He is currently at large."

"Wow," Evan blinked a number of times as he took in the news. "How's Chad?"

"Don't know yet but he looks a little better than when he first arrived, for what it's worth."

"Jesus, none of this makes any sense at all. I gotta tell ya."

"Can you tell me why?" Darrell waited for a clue into this mess.

"Uh, yeah...Where do you think he is now?" Evan

changed the subject.

"We don't know. That's why I am talking to you, actually. We've got an APB out on the car and we haven't heard anything yet. So, either he hasn't gone far or he's sticking to remote areas."

"Or maybe both." Evan offered but still wore a puzzled look.

"What do you mean?"

"Well...not sure." Evan wasn't sure how much he should say and Darrell was reading his apprehension. Evan was not quick to talk now that he realized that he was being interrogated about his friend.

Darrell waited for Evan to elaborate, but he didn't, so Darrell engaged again. "Yeah...look, I am going to be honest with you. I've got a real odd feeling about this whole thing. Maybe it's stupid instinct but here it is. Doug was definitely hiding something. At first he said an animal attacked his son, then he seemed unsure. The doctor determined that it was a beating, and not an animal attack. Now that would make complete sense with Doug's domestic violence background and all."

"Oh yeah, that." Evan said sarcastically.

"What?"

"Nothing, go on."

Darrell was getting agitated. "Alright Evan, I've had enough already of people holding back information on this thing. All I know is we've got a fourteen-year old kid in the hospital with internal injuries and the prime suspect stole a police car and is on the loose and nobody's talking. Now maybe this is just a cut and dry case, but maybe it isn't. But if nobody talks, well, I guess we'll never know!"

"He didn't do it." Evan quietly acquiesced.

"How do you know? I just told you about it."

"No, not that. I mean he never hit Ellen."

Something clicked in the puzzle in Darrell's mind with that statement. If Evan was telling the truth, then parts of Doug's behavior were starting to make sense, but Darrell was far from the solution. "Go on."

"She just used that in court. Doug's not that kind of guy. I honestly didn't think that she could pull that off and neither did Doug, but she was pretty pissed at him. I don't know if Ellen knew that she would obtain full custody of Chad as a result of it. I think she just wanted to make sure everybody thought he was an asshole."

"Why?"

"Because he was sleeping around on her."

Darrell sighed. That was one thing that was different
on the reservation. Living a lie. He knew so many
white folk that would walk around in their lives with
so many bullshit lies tied to them. It was hard for him
to imagine keeping a lie like that. How many people
did Ellen and Doug have to face with their lies hanging
over their heads? Not that his people were innocent,
but nobody would hide stuff like that. One thing it did
do was make his job easier on the rez. There were a
moderate number of crimes but very little detective
work. He rarely had to second guess a person or a
criminal act.

"Alright, let's think about this. According to what you
are saying, Doug is not the abusive type. Let's propose
Doug didn't hurt Chad. Ok, but somebody did."

"Why somebody? Didn't you say that Doug said an
animal attacked Chad?"

"Yeah, but his bruises weren't made by an animal.
There was a clear knuckle mark on his back and there
is not one scratch or claw mark on the kid's body. So
why would Doug lie and say an animal did it?"

"I don't know. I'm not the detective."

"Well neither am I, Evan. I'm a sheriff." There was a
pause as both men turned the situation over in their
own minds. Darrell spoke again, "Could he be
protecting someone?"

"I doubt it. He went up there with just Chad. I

sincerely doubt that he would cover for someone that he met up there. Hey stranger, beat up my son and I'll cover for you." Evan made a sarcastic gesture.

"You're right. That sounds pretty implausible." Darrell wanted to agree with him. Evan was Doug's friend and he wanted to make sure that he stayed on his good side, for if Doug was guilty, pleasantries wouldn't last for long and it would be a lot harder to extract information. "Where is *up there*?" Darrell asked.

"Up into the No Return. I should know. I gave him directions. There's an area up there off of a fire road that's got some great hunting. You would pretty much have to be blind not to kill anything."

"Anybody live there?"

"Nobody. It's got a spooky rap. There's like some bad Indian mojo or something..." Evan wasn't sure if he should have said that, thinking that Darrell might get offended.

Darrell didn't seem to care. "What, like old burial ground stuff?"

"Uh no ... I don't think so. It's not like it has that sacred thing. It's more like a stay away kind of feel."

"But you went up there no problem?" Darrell asked.

"Yeah, that's probably why the game is so good. No one goes there. I never went very far into the No

Return. I set up a blind a short distance away from my camp right off the fire road. The fire road connects to the Highway 21 about twenty miles north of town."

"Well, that's where he was last night. I caught up to him on the highway not too far from there."

"Hey, wait a minute...," a thought occurred to Evan. "Did you say that Doug broke out of jail?"

"Yeah."

"And then he stole your police car."

"Well, not mine, but my deputy's... but yeah."

"Well, if he didn't do it, why wouldn't he sit back in jail and wait for me to come forward and protest the abuse bullshit. He knows I would."

"Maybe he did it, Evan." Darrell acknowledged with regret.

"Or maybe he's going after the guy who did it." Evan stated.

CHAPTER SEVEN

The heat rose as the sun peaked in the sky. Even in early autumn, the temperatures in the mountain valleys could rise to eighty degrees. There was no wind to speak of either. No breeze to cool Doug as he trudged through the forest. The bugs around him hissed, as if they were burning in the warm sun. Heat distortion rippled the air across the earth before him.

The tracking was slow going. In some places the ground was too hard to allow for a good print, so he had to pay very close attention to signs of travel, like broken branches or crushed vegetation.

He passed through a meadow surrounded by rolling hills. The tracks lead straight across the meadow, crossing a small creek that was meandering its way through. The prints traveled right into the water and continued on the other side. Doug knelt down to touch the water. It was very cold. He wanted to drink from the creek but thought otherwise. Evan had told him about that weird virus or bug, or whatever it was. Maybe it wasn't in this stream, but then again maybe it was, Doug thought. He took some of the water and splashed it onto his face. The feeling was refreshing as the cool droplets trickled down his face onto his neck. But it could not satisfy his thirst. He was developing a sore throat. He didn't know if that was from the thirst or lack of sleep.

Doug continued on. The tracks crossed the creek once more. Or rather, the creek crossed the tracks. The creek was changing course through the meadow, not the tracks. The giant prints were straight, regardless of what obstacles lay before them.

As Doug looked back the way he had come, a thought occurred to him. He searched the ground along the creek bed for something to mark his current position and found a tall stick lying on the edge of the waterline. He took the stick and drove it directly into one of the prints on the side bank of the creek, leaving the stick pointing a few feet straight into the air.

Doug then backtracked about fifty yards, found another stick and used it to mark another track. He repeated his efforts another fifty yards back. Doug then crouched down, behind the last stick, and lined it up with the previous one further down the meadow. Once the two sticks were aligned on the same axis, the first stick he had placed one hundred yards away lined up perfectly with the other two. They were all in a straight line. Doug had noticed that the animal was moving in a relatively consistent direction before, but he wasn't sure until now that the thing was literally traveling in an absolute straight line.

Doug wanted to use this to his advantage. He knew that he would keep losing ground if he continued to track the animal the way he had been. Considering the stride length of the creature, it was doubtful that Doug could keep pace with it, even at a full run. It was a depressing thought. Nevertheless, Doug needed to find a way to pick up the pace. He crouched down again behind the stick and lined up the three sticks along the same axis. Doug then looked beyond the last stick to the territory ahead. A small group of trees lay in the distance, sitting alone in the middle of the meadow. They lined up perfectly with the sticks. He judged them to be a couple hundred yards ahead. He marched forward through the tall grass. Doug made a point not to look at the ground. He wanted to be right.

Doug arrived at the group of trees, and then began to search the ground. The prints showed up almost immediately, not five feet from where he standing. *I was right!* He wanted to try it again. He walked beyond the trees and placed a stick down once he found a track. He then followed the tracks as best he could through the meadow and dropped down another stick on a decent print. He walked another hundred yards and placed another marker. He crouched down and lined up the sticks. A straight line. *Yes!*

Doug grabbed the immediate stick and looked ahead. The meadow ended within a few hundred yards and started to climb a small, forested hill. He picked a spot halfway up the hill, where the trees cleared. It appeared to line up perfectly with his current direction, except that it climbed considerably in elevation. Doug was concerned that the tracks would not follow the straight line once the terrain became more difficult. Surely the creature wouldn't just walk right up a steep incline when it could easily go around it.

Doug walked forward to find out. Not having to scan the ground for clues, his walk evolved into a jog, but then slowed down again when the incline increased.

A few minutes later, an out-of-breath Doug came to the clearing on the hillside. He stopped and scanned the ground. He couldn't find any positive signs that the Bigfoot had traveled this way. The tall grass looked pristine and untouched. He circled the area, drawing doubt upon his theory as he found more undisturbed earth. If the creature had walked around the hill and went on, he wouldn't be able to trust that his theory could work, and he would have to resort to moving at the same slow find-every-track pace. Going back and lining up the sticks would then have all been a waste of time as well.

After making larger circles, Doug neared the edge of the clearing. It was there that the tracks reappeared. The footfalls had made giant depressions in the short grass. He stood in one of the tracks, both of his feet fitting within a single print. Doug looked back the way he had come. From the clearing, he could see the meadow below. It was difficult to spot, but he observed the tall stick he recently placed and then the group of trees beyond. It was more difficult to line them up because of the elevation change, but he felt comfortable enough that they were in a straight line with where he was, barring the change in height. *What a strange animal,* he thought. From the line he was on, he gauged where the next marker would be. He still had to finish climbing the hill he was on, so the best he could do was pick a target at the crest of the hill. He could see a tall pine at the top rising above the canopy. It didn't exactly line up but it was about twenty yards or so to the left of where he wanted to go. He made a mental note of that particular tree and started trekking upward.

The sweat began to pour down his face as he climbed. He was already missing the creek in the meadow. The moisture in the higher hills had drained down through the soil a long time ago. It was very dry up here. The air felt dusty. The whole place seemed like a tinderbox, ready to ignite.

Doug reached the peak of the hill. He scanned the area for the largest trunk. It ended up being about forty yards away from his search point, the tall pine reaching through the canopy into the sky above. Once at the tree, he walked twenty yards to the left of the trunk and looked for prints. He couldn't locate any definitive footprints in the dry earth, but he did find scrapings where the creature must have climbed to the hilltop. The marks were right where he would have expected them to be. He made a new bearing down the hill, this one not as far as the previous one because of the visibility in the dense vegetation. He could not see far enough into the woods to come up with a distant target. So he just took smaller increments as he relayed his way through the dense pine forest.

Minutes turned to hours and the terrain rolled on. Doug wanted to take a break, but it did not seem wise. The longer he procrastinated, the farther the creature would be away from him.

In mid-stride, Doug heard a snap of a large twig. It came from his right, in the thick underbrush. He stopped instantly, almost involuntarily. Even his breathing stopped as his subconscious drove him to be absolutely quiet. The sounds of the forest opened up to his ears. There was a bird singing in the distance, the flies swarming around him, and cicadas buzzing. Doug waited, perfectly still, waiting for whatever it was to make another sound. He heard nothing. It had to move sometime. What if it was the creature? What if it was looking at him right now? The thought gave him chills. He looked in the direction of the twig snap but saw nothing but dense forest. He bobbed his head around in hopes to see something at a different angle. He readied his gun. Minutes passed by. Nothing moved. He waited, but to no avail. Finally his patience wore out as he screamed at the forest.

"Hey! I know you're out there!" Doug yelled.

The forest rewarded him with more silence. Doug was tempted to fire the shotgun in the direction of the twig snap, thinking to drive the animal out. It would have been a waste of a shotgun shell if it wasn't the Bigfoot, but it seemed worth the risk. He fired one shot into the woods, bracing himself for what might come out.

Nothing moved except the bushes that were disturbed by the shotgun blast. Doug kept his eyes on the brush for any sign of movement, but it remained as still as it had been before. Frustration started to boil within him. He wondered if he had wasted a shell on the sound of a twig snap. The creature could have been ten miles away for all he knew, and he was shooting bushes. He could not wait anymore. Doug walked towards the area where he had heard the twig snap. For some reason, this required more courage. Following the animal's tracks was not as scary as going towards a sound in the bushes, bushes he had been walking through all day. Doug crept through the woods, keeping both hands on the shotgun. The high brambles scratched against his face but he didn't dare drop his guard. He walked farther, but nothing came out at him. He stopped and surveyed the area around him. There was nothing there.

Doug walked back to the trail with mixed emotions. In a way, he was relieved he hadn't found the creature. The memory of the creature standing in front of the fire was a frightful one. It had looked too powerful to be reckoned with, under any circumstances.

On the other hand, he was frustrated with how long it was taking to track this animal. He felt that he was running out of time, and he was not getting any closer.

Without the body, he had nothing. To return to
civilization now, Doug would be nothing more than an
escaped criminal. With seemingly no other options
before him, he moved on.

Hours later, the terrain changed once again. The
conifer forests were still present, but their branches
and needles had been stripped by fire. A forest fire
had obviously rolled through this area some time ago.
He was aware of the massive forest fires that had
gripped this part of Idaho a few years back. The woods
had become very dry one year, and it would not have
taken much to spark a blaze. Without warning, a
freak lightning storm ignited the forest in many areas.
A massive forest fire soon erupted. Forest servicemen
and firefighters could do very little with a blaze of such
magnitude. Thousands of square miles had burned
out of control in just a few days. All that was left were
the standing trunks of the tall pines. That's what
must have happened here. The place looked strange,
with the lack of vegetation on the trees increasing the
visibility through the forest immensely. A scalp with
thinning hair was the analogy that came to Doug's
mind. Other trees, almost as many as were standing,
had fallen and were lying all through the forest making
a cross hatching pattern. The ground was also
covered with a thin bed of burnt pine needles. The
lack of leaves and needles in the canopy brought very
little cover from the sun. The blazing heat poured
down from above, as the hot dry earth heated him
from below. Huge black flies swarmed around him
and paced with him like parasites as he moved. Doug
did not think much of them until one took a painful

bite at his hand. After that, he brushed them off continually, but that did not stop them from following him.

The opening up of the vista gave him an opportunity once again to search for more distant targets ahead for bearings. He made better progress now, but he wondered how long his luck, or his stamina, would hold out.

Darrell and Evan arrived at the campsite around two o'clock in the afternoon. They found the police car and knew immediately that they were on the right track. Darrell called Forsythe on the CB and instructed him to gather the search party at the sheriff's office and proceed to the campsite. Thinking ahead, Darrell and Evan had decided to bring T-Bone. The bloodhound was good at tracking down fowl that Evan had shot from the air, but she had never tracked a man before. Nevertheless, they had decided to bring her along, just in case she could be of any help. They brought T-Bone around and into the stolen police car, hoping she would catch the scent of Doug. The dog was excited but she wasn't focused, not knowing what to smell for.

Darrell looked around at the campsite. He noticed the broken glass, most likely from a window of the SUV. Whatever had happened the night before had probably happened here. But what? He also noticed the tire tread marks on the ground, heading out the way they had come in from. Darrell assumed that it was Doug hurrying to get Chad to the hospital. But why the broken glass? Had the assailant actually attacked them while they were in the car? Or, had an angry father smashed the window to get at his son, Chad?

The only other things of note were the tent and cooler bottom sitting near the smoldering ashes of a burned out campfire. The cooler top was oddly hanging from a rope, which was tied to a tall branch.

"I don't see your borrowed shotgun anywhere, Evan."

"Maybe it's by the blind. We might as well head up there. T-Bone definitely has enough of Doug's scent. We just have to make sure that she's focused enough to track his particular smell."

They made their way to the blind. Once there, the men noticed the empty beer cans. Doug and Chad had definitely been there, but that was about all they could determine.

"Well, what now?" asked Evan.

"Don't know. Why don't we circle around this area and see if we find anything. If we don't see anything or the dog doesn't pick up anything, then there's not much left to do other than wait for the search party...Hey, wait a minute. Here's a shotgun shell." Darrell pointed to the ground at the empty red plastic container.

"Well, he shot at something...or somebody." Evan

concluded.

"How do you know that these shells aren't yours?" Darrell asked.

"They are mine. Doug borrowed them from me. But I always clean up my shells. Always."

The two separated to cover more ground. After ten minutes, Darrell noticed the depression in the tall grass, and the dark stains in the center. Darrell called Evan over with T-Bone. As they approached, T-Bone started to trot slower and slower and then began to cower next to Evan's leg. At about ten feet away, T-Bone would not come any closer.

"What's the matter with your dog?" Darrell asked.

"Don't know. It's weird. I have never seen her behave like this. She's usually fearless. What's over there?"

"I don't know yet." Darrell took a closer look at the depression. "But there's definitely blood."

"Yeah, the question is whose?"

"We know it's not Chad's or Doug's because they didn't have any open injuries on them when they came to the hospital. And this blood looks about a day old so it couldn't be from Doug after he escaped, assuming he didn't get back here right away. I guess it's from some kind of animal that Doug shot."

"Maybe so, but where's the animal?"

"Exactly. And from the depression, it looked pretty big. What do you think it could have been?"

"I'd say either bear, elk, or maybe moose."

"So Doug shot the thing, and hauled it somewhere we haven't seen, and then Chad got attacked by some guy in the area near camp and then Doug gets his window smashed by the same guy as he pulls away in the SUV."

Evan shook his head. "This is really odd." Doug looked down at the whimpering T-Bone.

"Maybe we can track where Doug put the animal-kill?" Darrell suggested, looking at T-Bone.

Evan had to literally drag the bloodhound over to the depression. T-Bone was not happy, but still sniffed at the ground, reluctantly pulling in the scent of the animal.

"Why did you name your dog T-Bone?"

"Because she loves steaks, but whatever kind of animal this is, she definitely doesn't like it."

T-Bone was gaining courage as she started to make circles around the depression. She eventually arced out from the depression making her way toward the treeline, away from camp. They were not sure if she was following Doug's scent or the animal's, but they guessed it didn't matter. The two men followed the dog into the forest.

Pete Travers

CHAPTER EIGHT

The shadows crept along the land of the No Return as the sun continued on its inevitable arc across the sky. The heat began to slowly dissipate and was replaced by a welcomed breeze. Doug trudged along, taking solace when the sun would periodically break behind large cloud formations.

The woods were endless, endless beyond comprehension. The homogenous terrain made distances hard to gauge. Given the time he had spent traveling at a steady pace, Doug figured he must have covered a distance well past the full length of the town of Omah. But he had no destination. The length of his journey was not predetermined, so he did not know how to pace himself. If he moved fast, he would tire quickly, but at too slow of a pace, he might never reach his goal. The unknowns were battling in his mind, running so many scenarios of what may happen to him. Few of the possible scenarios sounded positive, and none of them made sense. The odds were terribly against him. Doug never considered himself a pessimist, but he was not the type to play against the odds. Oftentimes, he believed that satisfaction was simply not in the cards. In those times, he would usually give in and give up. He had a practical sense about things and lived his life by weighing the odds and taking the safe path. That's why he was so good with money. He didn't get caught up in the grandiose ebbs and flows of the stock market. He played it safe and didn't switch on a whim. It was a surefire way to keep from losing money, but the gains weren't much either.

By those measures, his current situation did not bode well. Doug was constrained by time, and he knew it. The police must have been on their way. It would probably take them awhile to find him here, but they would inevitably question Ellen as to his possible whereabouts, which would lead them to Evan. Evan was a good guy, but he wasn't about to defy the law and harbor a criminal. Not that he was a criminal, he hadn't done anything to anybody, but Evan wouldn't know that. No, his odds were not good. Even if Doug was not being chased by the police, he still didn't think he was going to find anything. *I mean c'mon, this is fucking ludicrous,* he thought. The creature could take a right turn over some hard earth or cross a river and he would be screwed. It might have even circled back. It could be behind him for Christ's sake. He visualized the giant creature standing behind him, waiting for Doug to turn so that it could bash his face in. The thought gave him goose bumps. He turned quickly to check, swinging the rifle around. The vista of the forest showed him nothing but plant life and dirt. There was nothing but woods. Maybe the creature was invisible, or even a shape-shifter that could blend into the natural surroundings. It must have had some skill like that. How else could something that big hide from man for so long? With all of the people that have camped, hiked, biked, and hunted in the woods, no one has been able to capture or kill one, or get one on film. Was he the first person to ever shoot and kill a Bigfoot? It seemed so unlikely. Some person in the past must have shot one or gotten one on film. *Maybe they have?* he thought. He remembered that film footage from the seventies of a Bigfoot walking across a creekbed. Maybe that was real. He had always thought it was a guy in a suit or something. That's what it looked like. But the proportions of the thing he saw were different. The one he saw was huge, and wide. Its shoulders were broad, bigger than any man alive. And the face was creepy, that huge brow with the deep-set eyes. He shivered just thinking about it.

It was about 4:00pm when Doug had to take a break. He had been trudging along for hours through the underbrush. The terrain was making a steady climb to higher altitudes. He figured that he must have gone about two thousand feet higher in the past three miles. All the while the tracks were making the same beeline toward the mountains. The creature must be incredibly strong to carry the young one for this long, he thought. Doug caught his breath once more and continued on.

Up a little ways, the terrain started to change. The dirt packed ground and underbrush were replaced by moss covered rocks and grass. He could hear water up ahead. A stream appeared. Its white waters were pouring down the creek bed, splashing on rocks and slowing in pools all down its course. It looked to be only a couple of feet deep at its deepest point.

Doug had tried to pay closer attention to the ground because the tracks were getting harder to read and, eventually, non-existent. Twenty yards from the stream, there was nothing but big rocks. His trail was gone. Where could it have gone? He wondered. It must have either crossed the stream or continued to travel along side it. Doug figured he would travel along the side, looking for any kind of clues to its presence. His luck was good up until now, but it wouldn't last forever. He knew that. There was nothing on the ground but rocks. What was he going to do?

And then he noticed it. Blood. There was some red color smeared on the rocks about 5 yards ahead from where he was standing. It was difficult to miss. The white washed rocks were stained with a maroon smear as if something had moved across it. His first thought was that it was the young one. Maybe the big one placed it on the rocks as it got some water. Or maybe it was another animal that it had killed. Were these things meat eaters? The thought gave him the chills.

It was getting darker, and Doug had to make a decision. Cross now, assuming the creature went to the other side and continued on, or stick with traveling up the river. What could he hope for if he stayed along the river? If the terrain did not change, he would just have to make the same guess sometime later as to when to cross. He thought back to the way the tracks appeared. They were in a straight line. So, based on the angle that they approached the river, they would have crossed somewhere around this location to make the same line. The straight-line behavior of the tracks didn't make any sense. Why were they so accurate? *What, does Bigfoot have a compass?* He laughed to himself, but it wasn't really that funny. Depression was starting to set in. He wasn't getting any closer to his goal. He was just going farther into the woods. It was looking hopeless. He was never going to find the creature if it did not want to be found. It was outpacing him, so he was not going to catch up to it. And what if he did find it? It wasn't going to amicably hand over its dead kid. And how would he carry the dead body? The young Bigfoot probably weighed more than him. *I'm pretty much fucked,* he thought.

Without warning, in a violent surge, Doug was whipped around and slapped onto a large rock below him. He landed square on his back so hard that the wind blasted out of his lungs. Standing before him was the creature, looming over him. A massive muscular arm reached out and placed a hand on Doug's chest, pinning him to the rock. The creature's human-like gargantuan hand spread across his entire chest pushing down hard enough that Doug couldn't breathe. The creature's coal-black face angled down and looked squarely into Doug's eyes. Doug was paralyzed in fear. He could not have moved even if the creature was not holding him down. Its face was contorted into an expression of unbridled rage. He was going to die. The creature's other hand came around and grabbed Doug's left arm around the bicep, which was still holding the shotgun. The creature's enormous chest flexed and Doug heard a sharp pop. Excruciating pain poured through his nerves from his shoulder. Doug lost bodily control. The thing was going to rip him apart. He blacked out.

Darrell and Evan followed T-Bone through the No Return. They passed through the same terrain that Doug had passed through hours earlier. The sun was dropping lower, casting a shadow in the lowland areas and valleys. Evan trusted T-Bone, and Darrell in turn had no choice but to trust the man and his dog. Doubt had been cast in both men's minds as they made their way deeper into the wilderness.

"Wow," Evan stated.

"What?" Darrell jogged ahead to Evan, thinking that he found something.

Evan had not found anything, but had drawn a conclusion. "Darrell, no one lives out here."

"What do you mean?"

"What I said. No one lives out here." Evan restated.

"I'm not following you." Darrell was confused. Evan was alluding to something, but he couldn't make the connection.

"No one lives out here. As in, the direction we are heading in is no-man's land. So why are we going in this direction?"

"Now I'm following you," Darrell thought. "Who could we be possibly chasing?"

"Right."

"Maybe it's a camper, or some other hunter like yourself?"

"I've been thinking about that, but it doesn't add up in my head. We haven't been on a trail or anything for miles."

Darrell finished Evan's thought, "Right, and who would trek for miles over untraveled terrain to find Doug and Chad camping, attack Chad and take off into the same wilderness? You are right, it's baffling."

"In your experience, do people run like this?" Evan asked.

"Yes, people do go remote when they are on the run. On the reservation, guys would do it all the time. They would retreat into the woods for weeks, and it was a pain in the butt to find them. The part that's odd is the circumstances of the crime, combined with where we are."

"What do you mean?" Evan asked.

"The crime occurred out in the middle of the woods, in a place that you only know about. I believe that Doug knows who or what did it, but did not want to say. He did, however, want to say that an animal attacked his son. Why would someone say that an animal attacked their son when they knew that a person did it?" Darrell was streaming out his observations and questions at the same time. "Something was definitely shot at in the clearing at the camp. Who or what got shot? Doug's trail led right from the clearing into the woods. Whatever got shot, spilled blood and managed to travel miles directly into the wilderness. All the while, Doug is flying out of here with Chad in the backseat of his SUV. But then, Doug breaks out of jail in the middle of the night to return to the camp, and then seems to track whatever it is, for a day across wild terrain. The doctor was sure that a man attacked Chad, but at this point, I'm not sure of anything."

While Darrell deliberated on the oddities of the situation, a dangerous thought occurred to Evan. What if Darrell concluded that Doug was guilty? Without himself and especially T-Bone, the sheriff would never have gotten this far. He could be potentially aiding the police in helping to capture his friend. He didn't think for a moment that Doug was guilty, but what if the police did not come to the same conclusion? Evan's options were to help Darrell follow the trail or to not cooperate. He could choose to not help and just walk away. The sheriff would be forced to wait for the search party. It would give Doug another half a day at least. But how much would that help Doug? If Evan quit now, would that cast more suspicion on Doug's character, like, if his buddy thinks he's guilty, why would anyone think he is innocent? Also, if he stopped now, it would take longer for anyone to reach Doug, and that looked like that was a bad thing. Doug was in danger. He was out here in the middle of the No Return, probably chasing some madman. Doug had no business being out in the wilderness. The only reason he was out here was because Evan had convinced him to go camping. He had to help. He owed it to his friend.

They crossed through the meadow and the fire-stripped valley. The temperature was a quite a bit cooler than when Doug had passed through, for the sun had dropped well past the valley walls. Only the bright hues of the sunset in the western sky were left now. As the color drained from the sky, so did Evan's hopes of finding his friend.

CHAPTER NINE

Doug woke up against the rock. The pain tore through his body from his shoulder. At least he was still alive. He opened his eyes and looked around. The creature was nowhere in sight. It was probably close, waiting to finish him off. *Go ahead,* he thought. The pain was unbelievable. His arm was just dangling off of his body. He felt like he was going to puke. He had never had a dislocation before but he knew he had to pop it back in. *Or maybe I could just blow my head off with my good arm.* There wasn't much point now to going on. He knew that he didn't have much of a chance of continuing the search. That thing had come up on him in a clearing by a river in broad daylight and he didn't even see it.

Just then he noticed the smell. It was an awful stench, somewhere between rotting garbage and horrendous body odor. He looked down and noticed a large moist spot on the front of his pants. *Oh God, I must have shit my pants.* After a moment, he realized that he hadn't, only pissed himself. But what was that smell? It must have been the animal. Between the smell and his shoulder, Doug couldn't overcome the nausea, and heaved forward, regurgitating on himself.

Doug, having thrown up, felt considerably better, enough to clear his mind and think, as much as he could with a completely dislocated shoulder. Jesus, there was so much pain that he was doing everything he could to keep from crying. *What do I do? Pop it back in? ... How?* The nausea was rolling back in. He wished the creature had finished him off. *That stupid thing.* It was fucking with him. *It knows it has me, and it just decided to hurt me as opposed to killing me. It probably killed Chad and now it wants to torture me. I didn't know that I had shot at its god-damned son!*

Anger was building in Doug, both at the creature and himself. He had to do something. Doug turned his body around to face the large flat rock he had passed out on. He took a couple of big breaths. He leaned back, lining up his wounded shoulder with the flat face of the boulder. He torqued his body and slammed his shoulder square against the rock as hard as he could.

"Fuck!" Doug screamed. He collapsed back against the rock bed, his shoulder still dangling to his side. It did not go in.

It took all of Doug's remaining energy to get back up to his knees. He had to attempt it again. He had never been in this much pain in his entire life. He didn't want to have to try this again, so he put all of his energy into it. Either way he figured he would pass out. He swung around screaming as he made another attempt.

It went in. There was still so much pain but he knew that the ball of his shoulder bone fell back into its socket. A wave of blackness rolled over Doug's consciousness. As Doug passed out again, his last thoughts were that the creature would probably just dislocate his shoulder again, while he lay there.

Darrell and Evan had followed T-Bone through the underbrush in the darkness. It was a new moon that night so there was absolutely no light peeking through the tree canopy. Only Darrell's flashlight gave them any light. They moved slowly until Darrell decided to stop as they crossed a muddy flat. He saw something.

"Hold on Evan, I think I see a footprint." Darrell could make out the distinct shape of a boot on the ground. It had to be Doug's.

"Can you tell how fresh it is?" Evan asked, rasping, still breathing heavily from their jog through the underbrush chasing after T-Bone.

Darrell sighed. This was the kind of stuff that he wished he had paid more attention to when he was growing up on the reservation. Something about the moisture levels in the prints relative to the ground could determine the freshness of the tracks. He could not recall the specifics. "Well, I really don't have a solid feel for it, but my guess is that the tracks are about a half-day old."

"What's your guess based on?" Evan asked, curious as to how Darrell arrived at that answer.

"The Spirits told me." Darrell said.

Evan tilted his head to the side and gave Darrell a dubious look.

"Just kidding... Not much really, other than there is still more moisture in the print than in the surrounding mud, which means that it's definitely within a day. The half-day is just a guess within that timeframe." Darrell admitted.

"At least it's within a day." Evan was impressed. He felt that he was a pretty good hunter but he realized that he knew very little about track forensics.

T-Bone came up between the two and started sniffing another track cautiously, of which Evan took notice. Evan cocked his head at what he could see of the new track at the perimeter of the flashlight beam.

"Uh Darrell...shine your light on that track T-Bone's sniffing."

"What?..." Darrell started to ask but he then saw why Evan had stopped to notice it. He centered the beam on the track and both men took a step closer. A bare human shaped footprint lay on the ground, a rectangular sole with five distinct toe prints in the soft mud.

The only problem with the print was that it was about eighteen inches long and about a half a foot wide.

"Holy shit." Evan said.

Just then, a roar echoed through the woods. The source was miles away, but it was so loud that it could be heard echoing off the mountains. It sounded like a human scream, but it was too powerful, too deep. It came from the direction of where the tracks lead.

"Holy shit." Both men said in unison.

Doug awoke to the blasting roar. The creature was close, but he couldn't determine its position because he was completely blinded by the night. Absolute blackness dominated his vision. He couldn't see his own hands in front of his face. The hairs on the back of his neck rose up and he started to sweat from fear. He was totally outmatched and totally out of his element. The Bigfoot was circling him, as he could hear its giant footsteps. It must have been staying in the tree cover as its feet landed on twigs and underbrush.

"What are you waiting for?!" Doug cried out defiantly.

Silence. Minutes passed by. Not a sound emerged from Doug's surroundings. What was it doing? Doug didn't move and just tried to listen. He slowly brought up the shotgun with his good arm and got to a kneeling position. Doug used the shotgun as a crutch and slowly stood up. He brought his bad arm around to hold the underbelly of the shotgun barrel. The pain was still very much there, but at least he could use the arm. From his elbow down to his hand, there was severe numbness. He couldn't feel his last two fingers. He probably had nerve damage. Not like it mattered anymore.

Doug heard a noise in the brush behind him, about ten feet away. He turned and fired the shotgun blindly in that direction. In the faint instantaneous flash of the shotgun blast, all that he could see in the direction that he had fired was the tree-line. No sign of the creature. Another sound came from the opposite direction. He spun and fired again, feeling the painful recoil of the gun in his shoulder. Again, there was nothing to see but the edge of the woods.

Doug started screaming into the forest again. Nothing could have moved that fast. Not even this creature. There was another sound this time, off to his left. A splash in the water. He fired again. This time in the faint light, he got a clear image of the riverbed and the surrounding area. Not a sign of the creature. No way. It had to be something other than footfall. He reloaded the shotgun. He had seven shells left. He knew because he had counted earlier. Seven shells. Was this thing trying to draw his fire and waste his ammunition? *Nah*, he thought, *animals aren't that smart.*

But was this just an animal? He had heard of Bigfoot before. He had watched some of those old 70's documentaries on Bigfoot, of how they said they were half-man, half-ape and how in some eye-witness accounts they had shown reasoning intelligence, and specifically, skill at hiding from man. Doug just thought that was some bullshit excuse made up by the show because they hadn't found one yet, but he was not sure now.

One thing he did know for sure: This thing was trying to confuse him of its whereabouts. So he would wait until he had a better shot. *A better shot?! When would that be, in the morning when there was better light?* That was laughable as he thought about it. He wasn't going to last the night. Doug was circling backwards but realized all he was doing was making noise. Circling was pointless if he couldn't see anything. He stopped moving completely. He couldn't use his eyes so he had to rely on his ears. This thing out there was moving easily through the woods so it could obviously see in the night. The frightening part was that it seemed to know that Doug could not. He wished he had brought the flashlight. Minutes passed by. Not a sound came from the woods around him. Maybe it had gone away? Something that big couldn't walk silently. There was just no way.

And then all hell broke loose. It was about fifty yards

away, clearly within the dense tree brush. The
creature was moving like a bulldozer, plowing through
the trees, roaring at the top of its lungs. Tree limbs
were snapping like they were twigs. It was moving
closer to him. God, it was awful. Doug had barely
enough wherewithal to lift the gun and aim it in the
direction of the source. *This is it*, he thought. *I am
going to die.* It was getting closer. The Bigfoot was
about thirty yards away now. Doug lifted the shotgun,
bracing the butt of the shotgun squarely into his
shoulder, the barrel out towards the sound. Twenty
yards away now. *Ok Doug, you're going to go out
blazing.*

Doug blasted the shotgun. The light flashed in the
direction of the charging animal, but showed only
trees. But it was in there, he knew it, and it was still
charging and howling at a deafening level. Fifteen
yards. Doug fired again. And again. Doug's shotgun
blasts ripping through the forest. He reloaded quickly
and fired again. Again. It had to be at the tree line
now, and gave no evidence that it was slowing down.
It was tearing through the trees. He must have hurt it.
He must have. Doug blasted the shotgun again.

And then it stopped. Doug was waiting for the animal
to come down on him and crush him. He listened and
waited for his own death. *Come on fucker, end it.* A
minute passed by and nothing. Another minute.
Doug was shaking, his gun still pointing in the same
direction. *Jesus, what's going on?!* There was just
absolute silence. The giant beast could have been
standing right in front of him and he wouldn't know.

Maybe it was. He could fire his last shell. There was
no sound, so it could not have moved. Maybe he killed
it? He had just pumped enough lead into the woods to
kill a family of them. But he didn't hear anything. No
birds or insects. Just the sound of the moving water
behind him. Eventually it had to make a noise.
Nothing could be this quiet. Minutes passed by.
Nothing. He must have killed it.

What should he do now? He couldn't go looking for it.
Not in this darkness. Doug would have to wait until
first light and then go find it. And then what should
he do when he found it? Haul an eight hundred
pound animal ten miles back to the car with his one
good arm? *Oh well, I've gotten this far. I'll figure it out
in the morning.* He guessed he would probably look to
be a pretty ugly sight when he got back; his pants all
pissed on, his shirt covered in puke, and he stunk.
Boy, did he stink. The smell had almost gotten worse.
It *was* worse. He felt a drop of water land on the back
of his neck. He felt the hot breath of something
behind him.

And then Doug was flying through the air, hit so
strongly from behind that he felt like he had been bent
in half. He hurtled through the blackness and landed
hard, his head banging on a rock. He lost
consciousness immediately upon impact.

Darrell and Evan heard the multiple shotgun blasts. It
wasn't very easy to determine the exact direction

because of the echo, but it was definitely coming from the east, towards the mountains.

"C'mon T-Bone!" Evan riled up the bloodhound. The men followed at a measured run. It was really hard to move because there was only the flashlight's beam for visibility. There was no path to follow. Evan repeatedly tripped as he maintained the hold of T-Bone's leash.

"How far do you think Doug is away from us?" Darrell asked through heavy breaths.

"Not sure. I figure at least five miles. If we keep going we might be able to get there by first light."

"I don't think we can keep up a jog for another five miles. That's a long way." Darrell looked down at T-Bone. "Thank God we got your dog. Smart move." The two men jogged side by side with Darrell holding the flashlight and Evan holding the leash. After twenty minutes, they had to slow down. It was too tiring to run continuously. They walked for another ten minutes, catching their breath in the hopes of picking up the pace again. As soon as they felt rested, the men moved forward again at a slow jog.

After about an hour, T-Bone got excited, and yapped wildly as she made her way down an angled hill into a low-plateaued area, dense with Douglas firs. They were getting closer to something. Another ten minutes and both men stopped and reloaded their shotguns. T-Bone was highly agitated. It was an understood situation. They both knew what they could be up against now, and they were not taking any chances.

Evan held T-Bone at bay with one arm and his shotgun poised in the other. Darrell was doing the same respectively with shotgun and flashlight. T-Bone stopped barking now and moved cautiously and determinedly through the underbrush. She wasn't sniffing anymore. She had found her target.

Evan whispered, "We are close. You ready?"

"Ready," Darrell whispered back.

Evan let go of T-Bone's leash and she immediately dashed into the copse of trees. There was a commotion as branches shook in the vegetation before them. As both men stood ready to fire, out came a wild flash of movement. Evan fired only once out of reflex but Darrell put his barrel down. It was a wild animal all right, but not what they were hoping to find. A jumbled mass of moving feathers scrambled out of the trees before them. It was a turkey. The large bird bounced twice, spread its wings and nervously took flight, angling away from the hunters. Once it was fully airborne, it became silent as it drifted away, beyond the reach of the flashlight beam and into the night.

"Shit." Evan spat, realizing that they had been chasing the wrong scent.

The quiet noises of the woods quickly returned. Evan

shook his head in disappointment.

Darrell consoled him. "That's alright Evan. You said your dog chases fowl for you, and she did exactly that. I just wonder how long we have been off the trail."

"Ah shit, who knows," Evan interjected. Just then T-Bone emerged out the woods, thinking herself triumphant.

"Let's backtrack as far as we can, but sooner or later we should probably crash for the night. We can make faster progress in the morning."

"Fuck." Evan was still pissed. "This could have set us back hours."

They trekked their way back the way they had come, and in the dark, it was slow going. Only the trail they had made previously was their ticket back. They moved slowly, which gave them the breath to talk. Evan asked a question that he wasn't sure if it was smart to ask, but at this point in time, he felt it couldn't hurt anything.

"You think Doug is innocent?"

"Yes." Darrell quickly responded. "I kind of had an idea a little while back. Actually, ever since I talked to his ex-wife. She was totally surprised when Doug was accused of violence, and I actually believed Doug when he said an animal attacked his son. When we saw the print, everything finally started to fall in place, as implausible as Bigfoot might seem."

"Ok, so ... what do you know about Bigfoot?" Evan cautiously asked.

"A little bit, I guess you could say, if there is anything to know. We've had all kinds of stories on the reservation, but most of them are old tales. The elders said that the Giant Ones were once in our area but they had left to go to the spirit world for their land was diminishing."

"Interesting. What do you think that means?" Evan asked.

"Most of the tales of the past are based in truth, Evan. If the elders say that the Giant Ones left, then that means to me that they were once here. Meaning: they existed somewhere in the deeper wilderness. As big as Montana is, most of it was converted to farmland when the settlers moved in and did their thing. You take away the land, you take away the animals, and the spirit world for that matter. But central Idaho is a different story. This wilderness here seems to be pretty untouched."

"It is. So you believe in Bigfoot?"

"Yeah, but that's not really why."

"Then why? Because of Doug? Because of the tracks?"

"No, because I've seen one before."

Evan stopped in his tracks. "You're shitting me?!"

"No, I am not." Darrell paused. "This is just between you and me, OK?"

Evan sensed his unease. "Hey, don't worry. Who am I going to tell? About the only friend I have other than T-Bone is somewhere out in these woods and I don't think HE is going to laugh at you."

"Yeah, probably not. But believe it or not, it's not so much about Bigfoot that I am worried about. You see, it's a different world on the reservation. As much as the white man, no offense, has tried to destroy the culture of my people, it is still very much intact, but it's kept very secret. Most of our ceremonies are behind closed doors and at night, and no one mentions them off the rez. Sure, we have our token stuff that we invite white folk to, like the Pow-Wow in Boise, or the San Geronimo festival down South, but that's all really to sell crafts and make money. They don't have any strong spiritual meaning anymore. The real stuff no one knows about."

"Cool."

"Yeah, in a way it is." Darrell nodded. "The preservation of our culture is paramount to the elders, and they believe that secrecy is the best chance to keep the old ways alive."

"That's not really that hard to argue with, all things considered." Evan acquiesced.

"Yeah, it's just the debate occurs in whether secrecy fosters segregation." Darrell waved his hand to change the subject back. "Regardless, when I was about eleven years old, we were having one of our ceremonies that I figure I won't tell you the name, but it's basically a reverence of nature kind of thing. It was the first time I got to go to it, kind of a manhood thing, so I was pretty excited. It took place at midnight, where all the men of the tribe, I think there were about twenty of us, gathered in the longhouse, which is essentially a tent with a square wooden frame, only much bigger than a teepee. Walking into the longhouse with my dad, I noticed a huge elk kill outside hanging over the fire pit on a spit. We got inside and closed all of the doors and passed around the pipe and started to chant in the old tongue. This stuff goes on for hours and with all the smoke and chanting going on, you start to trip out. You get into this kind of half dream state, when you are not sure what's really going on."

Evan was listening intently as the two stumbled along. Only then did Evan observe that the sheriff spoke very much like a white-blooded American. He wondered if Darrell spoke like that intentionally to help assimilate himself into the white man's culture. He doubted that Native Americans used phrases like "trip out" to describe ceremonies on the reservation.

"At the time, I swear I could hear something outside, but I wasn't sure. I remember getting a little dizzy, but

I didn't want to leave because I would look like a wimp, but then I definitely heard something outside. I hadn't seen a bear yet, so I figured I would take a quick peek. I opened the flap and stuck my head outside. Movement turned my head towards the campfire and I saw it outlined by the fire."

"Bigfoot?"

"Yeah, it was huge. The mass of the thing was towering over the elk kill. It was eating the elk. Its back was to me so I couldn't see its front side, but I could definitely tell what it was. But then I think it heard me or something because then it turned and looked right at me." Darrell paused with a quick shudder, thinking about the moment that occurred twenty-five years ago. "I'll never forget the look in its face. It growled at me and I lost it. I started screaming. I wanted to go back into the tent but the way was blocked as my father was coming out to see what was going on. The thing ran right by me as it stormed into the woods, in flight. I was so scared, I could not move. I have never felt so helpless in my entire life, and I never want to feel that way again. The thing was gone in moments. For some reason, even though I was the only one that saw it, they knew what I saw. It was like they thought I was privileged."

"Holy shit, I wish I could see one."

"No you don't, Evan. I can vouch for that. Not at night, not like that. I had nightmares for the next ten years. I have never been able to get that thing out of my head. There is something so primal about it. More intelligent than any other animal, and much more powerful. The face, dark with those coal-black eyes." Darrell closed his eyes, pondering the vision from his past. "Trust me. You do not want to meet up with one on a dark night alone."

"You mean like Doug?" Evan stated, reminding himself of the current situation.

"Yeah, and if my guess is right, he's got an angry one out there. I think he might have taken a shot at one, and I think it might have retaliated on Chad. That would explain a lot of things right now. It would never hold up in a court of law, but I think Doug knew that, which is why he had so much trouble relaying any facts about the animal that attacked Chad. An animal that no one thinks really exists."

"Well, at least he's got a shotgun with him, so he's got some defense anyway." Evan admitted.

"It's not enough." Darrell admitted.

The two men decidedly picked up the pace again.

CHAPTER TEN

It was very early morning at the Omah hospital. Chad's room was dimly illuminated by the open door to the lit hallway. Ellen was sitting in a chair, asleep with her head resting on Chad's hospital bed. Chad was sweating, tossing and turning with his eyes closed. He was having some kind of nightmare.

Chad screamed "Dad! Help!" and lifted up into a sitting position. Ellen woke up and grabbed Chad to console him. Chad reacted, disoriented and pulled away screaming, thinking it was his assailant. Ellen desperately tried to console him, assuring him that he was not in danger.

"Don't worry Chad, you're OK. I'm here."

Chad regained a measure of coherence. "Where's Dad?"

"Lie down, Chad. You need to rest. You've been in a

coma for a day." Ellen thought about that statement, wondering if resting after a coma was a good idea.

"Where's Dad, Mom?" Chad asked again.

"Chad..." Ellen paused. "Your Dad broke out of jail last night."

"Jail? Why is Dad in jail?"

"Because they think he hurt you." Tears started to well up in Ellen's eyes. Guilt overcame her very quickly.

"Mom, he didn't hurt me. He saved me."

"I know, I know. Just relax. Everything is going to be alright."

Just then, the nurse came in, responding to the screams from earlier.

Ellen attempted to calm the nurse. "He's OK." Chad started to get dizzy and laid back down, his eyes closing as he was drifting back asleep.

"Well, let me do my job and make sure." The nurse gently reminded Ellen. She walked around to the other side of the bed and checked the readout machine attached to Chad via a number of tubes and wires. The nurse was satisfied and smiled to Ellen. Ellen put a gentle hand on Chad's forehead and then turned back to the nurse. "Do me a favor. I need to get a hold of the sheriff. Can you do that for me?"

The nurse thought about asking why for a moment, but then resigned to minding her own business. "Sure," said the nurse as she walked out of the room. Ellen returned to looking at Chad, and laying her hand on his chest to feel his heartbeat. It was steady and strong.

The nurse returned, pointing to the phone in the room with the flashing light. "The police station is on line one. I couldn't get the sheriff. He wasn't there, but I got the deputy."

"Thanks."

"No problem. I am going to call the doctor. He's going to want to drop by and take a look at Chad. Congratulations."

"Thanks again." They shared smiles.

Ellen picked up the phone. Forsythe was waiting on the other end.

"Hello, Ms. Loncar. We were just heading out the door. The search party is ready to look for your ex-husband. The sheriff and Evan Ratcliffe are already out there with a head start. He won't escape," Forsythe reported.

"Good, Evan's with him. That's good. Hey, I need you to do me a favor."

"Sure thing, what?" Forsythe asked.

"I need you to tell the sheriff that it looks like Chad is going to be fine. He just woke up a few minutes ago." Ellen looked down at Chad. Chad's eyes were open, and he was listening as intently as he could.

"Well, that's good news."

"Make sure you tell the sheriff so that he can tell Doug when he finds him."

"Ok...Why?" Forsythe did not understand. He thought that Ellen was showing a lot of concern for a guy she should be hating right now.

"Just do it, please."

"Not sure why you'd care, but fine. Your life. I'm going to be communicating with him in a few moments. I'll tell him then."

"Thank you. Bye." Ellen finished the conversation and looked down at Chad. His eyes were closed again, but he was smiling.

It was the middle of the night, and the three companions were not making very good progress. They had been hiking for over twelve straight hours and fatigue was taking its toll. T-Bone had never tracked a scent for this long, and she was losing focus, wandering in zigzag fashion, constantly looking back as if to say, *When can we stop?* Both Darrell and Evan were having difficulty staying alert. The main thing keeping them awake was the treacherous terrain ahead of them. The difficult landscape, combined with the lack of light, made their movement that much more tiring.

Darrell was awakened from his walking trance by a faint sound. "Do you hear that?" he asked Evan.

"Do I hear what?" Evan groggily responded.

"That noise. It sounds like boiling water." Darrell stopped in his tracks to clear the sounds of his own movement.

Evan stopped as well and listened. "Yeah. I hear it." And then a moment later, the sound jogged his memory. "Oh yeah."

"What?" Darrell asked.

"It's a hot spring. Come on, let's find it." Evan said as he grabbed the flashlight and wandered in the direction of the noise. Darrell grew concerned that Evan was getting delirious from the lack of sleep. Why would a spring be so important when they had crossed over a creek just a few hours ago? He followed the beacon of the flashlight, having no choice other than standing in the dark.

He found Evan standing at the edge of a pool

surrounded by large rocks. The water at the center of the ten foot wide pool was being disturbed by hot bubbling water emanating from a hole at the bottom.

Evan muttered. "Do you smell anything?"

"No, why?"

"Perfect." Evan said as he dropped down to water's edge and cupped his hand into the liquid and drank from his hand. "You thirsty?"

Only then did Darrell realize how long ago it was since he'd had anything to drink. It had been in the morning. "Yes, I am." He dropped down to the edge and drank as well. The warm water was refreshing despite its temperature. He drank again.

"Drink up. Have as much as you can. No telling how long we will be out here." Evan advised.

"Why, what's the big deal, the water is everywhere out here?"

"Because of giardia. It's a parasite that lives in the waterways in the wilderness. If you drink it, it can make you really sick for a long time."

Darrell was ready to spit out the water in his mouth.

"But the good thing is that this is a hot spring, and we are up pretty high here."

"So."

"So, giardia comes from fecal matter from livestock and people. It gets into the rivers down south from the sewage runoff. You shouldn't drink the river water. But a hot spring is different. Hot springs don't have giardia in them."

"Why not?" Darrell asked.

"For two reasons, giardia is killed by boiling water. And by the bubbles coming up, you can tell that this water source starts as steam, so any giardia that would get into this pool would die. The second reason is that hot springs sources are very deep, way down into the earth where the rocks are molten. Water, way down below, comes in contact with the rocks, turns into steam and makes its way to the surface. If it is hot, that means it is deep, which means it is safe. The only thing you have to worry about is the sulfur content, but if you can't smell that rotten egg smell, then it's fine."

"Great." Darrell took another gulp.

"Central Idaho is littered with hot springs, more than any other state. They kept some of the frontiersman alive during the winter months." Evan added.

The two men sat at the water's edge and T-Bone came up to join them. She took a long welcome drink from the spring. Darrell patted T-Bone while she drank. "How far do you think we are from Doug?"

"Difficult to say. Could be one mile, could be ten. I just don't know how well we are doing on the scent." Evan nodded over to T-Bone in a way where he wanted to make sure that the dog didn't know that they were talking about her. "She's never tracked something this far, and now we are backtracking over our own scent to get back to where we lost the trail in the first place. We've been going at least twice as slow as when we were tracking during the day. And I'm not sure if we are going to be able to find the point where we lost the trail in this darkness." Evan paused. "I wonder if we should rest until daylight."

"I've been thinking the same thing for the past two hours. I know how you feel," the sheriff assured him.

"No you don't sheriff. Doug's not your friend. He's mine!" Evan raised his voice. "And I'm the one who sent him out here in the first place. And now Chad is in the hospital and Doug is in the middle of the wilderness with some kind of fucking monster..."

Darrell cut him off, "Which is not your fault, Evan." Darrell had been thinking about Evan's mindset before he had voiced his concerns. "Are you going to take the blame for Doug encountering a sasquatch? Like you would have known that, or ever guessed that an encounter with a sasquatch would ever be a possibility. Come on, Evan. Don't blame yourself. The circumstances are beyond crazy."

Evan was quiet. Darrell's words were making sense,

but Evan couldn't help but feel responsible. He took some water and splashed his face. "I have never been in a situation like this before."

"What do you mean?"

"I feel like Doug's life is in our hands, and stopping for rest seems so weak, especially if we found out he was a mile away, face down in a ditch. But we are just not making any progress, and if we don't rest now, we'll be dogging it all tomorrow."

Darrell solved the dilemma by looking at his watch. "Evan, it's four in the morning. We only have two hours until daylight anyway. Let's get some rest and pick up at first light."

Evan thought for a moment. "Two hours won't set us back too far, and we could use the rest."

Evan looked down at T-Bone. The dog was already asleep.

A caravan of trucks traveled down the now well-traveled fire road, making their way to the campsite. Forsythe, in the lead truck of three, hailed Darrell at 6:00am once he believed he was within reasonable range.

"Come in Darrell, this is Forsythe, please respond. Do you read?"

No response. Forsythe waited a few minutes and tried again. He was getting static. The caravan was almost at the camp. The walkie-talkie then chirped and stuttered, giving the indication that someone was trying to respond.

"Th ... Darell ... ver." the response came back littered with static.

"This is Forsythe. We are almost at the camp. It will be daylight soon."

"Cannot ..ear .. repeat." The response came back. The signal was fading in and out and was getting worse.

"Almost at the camp, over."

"We ... day ahead ... east."

Forsythe remembered. "Chad's OK."

"...leez .. peat." Came a barely imperceptible response.

"Chad is OK! Chad is OK!" Forsythe said. "Any sign of Childress? Over."

And then all Forsythe could get was static.

"Was that our wake-up call?" Evan asked with his eyes still closed.

"It sounds like Chad is OK." Darrell relayed to Evan in the early light of pre-dawn.

"That's a relief. It sounds like you were having trouble with that thing. You out of range or something?" Evan groggily asked as he sat up from his earthen bed.

"Doubt it, especially if the search party is at the campsite by now. The range of these things is about 15 miles, so they should be well within range." Darrell looked around. "These mountains must have a lot of iron in them. I think its screwing with the signal."

"It's going to be hard for them to gain ground without communicating with us."

"I would agree. Not that it matters that much." Darrell relinquished. "They are a day behind anyway. By the sounds of gunfire last night and those howls, I think WE need to catch up with Doug as quickly as possible."

"I hear ya. Well, lets hope T-Bone doesn't find any more fowl."

Darrell took one last drink from the spring. He wanted to imbibe as much as he could. Hopefully Doug was not far off, but if he was, the water would be necessary. A thought occurred to him.

"Does Doug know about giardia?" Darrell asked.

Evan dropped his head and breathed a sigh. "Yes and no."

"What?"

"Yes, he knows about giardia and knows not to drink the water. The problem is that he doesn't know what to drink. He doesn't know about the hot springs. If he has been out here this long, then he better drink something, or he'll die of thirst. Giardia is a nasty thing, but it won't kill you." Any positive attitude that had resulted from the rest, died in Evan's mind with that thought. He felt that there was nothing more to be said on the subject and urged T-Bone to find the trail once more.

In the dim light, they moved much faster, and the two men were able to confirm that they were on the right track, from the prints of their own boots going in the opposite direction.

In a few hours, they had arrived, at least they guessed, at the point of the diversion. T-Bone had changed direction and her mannerisms reverted back to a more subdued behavior. She was behaving the way she had before. She did not want to track the creature. They renewed their hunt with earnest, but a nagging feeling was gnawing at both men's minds that they might have lost a lot of precious time and that it might be too late.

CHAPTER ELEVEN

Doug woke up face down on the rocks. He had been unconscious for hours. His first thought upon waking was that it was all a dream. The attack, Chad being hurt, everything had been imagined. None of it really happened. But reality slowly came back to him. His psyche tried to fight the truth, but it was overcome by the anguish wrought by the events from the previous two days. Doug could not hide from the truth. He would never be able to hide from it. Doug was a fugitive, and a monster wanted to kill him. The same monster that may have killed his son. His son may be dead. Doug did not want to be awake. He wanted to drift away, away from everything, but the pain stopped him and pulled him back to the present.

Doug had a splitting headache. His back felt like somebody had taken a sledgehammer to it. He slowly kneeled up, grimacing, and touched his forehead. There was dried up blood on his fingers. The moments from the night before came back to him. *Jesus, what a night,* he thought. His arm was still extremely sore and as he tested it, he found that it had very limited range. He couldn't hold the shotgun with it, so he had to use his good arm. He got up dizzily and looked around.

With the light coming through the canopy, Doug could see the path where the Bigfoot had charged him. He moved closer and saw the path of destruction. It was impressive. Saplings were snapped in half about three feet up as if they were twigs. *How am I not dead?* Doug asked himself.

He figured that he had better take his chances in daylight because he was not going to last through another nightly encounter with the creature. He sneezed and noticed how cold he was. The temperature must have dropped in the night. He felt a cold coming on and all he had was a thin jacket.

He walked unsteadily around the rock bed, wandering towards the other side of the stream to the riverbank on the far side. The thing must have continued on to wherever it was going. He scanned the soft muddy bank for signs of tracks. There wasn't much of anything. He moved up the bank for another one hundred yards and finally found something. A pile of fresh dirt at the bottom of the bed, as if something had climbed up and agitated the steep incline. He noticed however, that the way ahead was covered with brambles. It was as if the creature had disappeared into a wall of thick brush.

"What the..?" Doug blurted.

He was confused. The bushes were five feet high,
perched on a steep incline. There was no way that the
creature could have jumped over the thorny bushes.
Almost as an afterthought, he pulled on the brambles.
To Doug's surprise, the bushes came towards him
easily. It was because the brambles were not rooted to
the ground. He could see the soft muddy bank
continue up under where the brambles were located,
showing that no plants had taken root in the mud. Not
recently anyway. The brambles were not growing here,
they were placed here, right over the giant footprints.
The thing was covering its tracks! He could see where
it had pulled the brambles at the root farther up the
trail and laid them down at the bank base. *So, you're
a smart fucker. Well, not smart enough to fool me.*

The creature showed clear signs of intelligence. Doug
could have dismissed the creature's tactics from last
night as chance from a more instinctive animal. But
last night's behaviors now combined with its ability to
think to cover its own tracks was too much to be
ignored. This thing was smart, or at least smarter
than a typical animal. Doug could only think that
when it went after Chad, it had done so by making a
decision. Doug thought of Chad lying on the ground at
the campsite. He was probably dead. There was no
way that Chad could have survived an attack if the
animal wanted to kill him. He felt so ashamed. Why
couldn't it have been him that died and not Chad?
Chad didn't do anything. Why hadn't the animal come
after him while he was at the dead body? Doug was

the one who shot the younger Bigfoot. But there was no way the adult creature could have known that he was the one who pulled the trigger. Unless, of course, the giant beast had been watching them all along. That gave him the creeps just thinking about it. But how would a Bigfoot even know what a gun is? It made Doug's head spin trying to ponder the possibilities. But if Chad was dead, none of it seemed to matter that much. It was all such a waste.

So what do I do now? Doug thought to himself. He could track the thing again, but he would never be able to drag its dead body back. It was too far. And he only had one shotgun shell left. He couldn't go back now. He had nothing, except for a dislocated shoulder and wrenched back. He would go back just to go to jail for a long, long time.

He was not going to jail. Whatever he did, he was not going to jail. *I'd rather kill myself than sit there for the next 50 years rotting in a cell. Keep moving.* He climbed up the embankment and continued on.

Doug traveled for about an hour until he could hear the sounds of moving water. The constant deep noise of rushing water up ahead sounded more powerful than what he had encountered before. The terrain was dropping sharply, and through the cracks in the trees, he could see the raging torrent below. Its white waters were surging over the rock riverbed. This was a bigger waterway than the one he had passed through earlier. It appeared to be a main fork of the Salmon River. The giant boulders stood against the mighty flow, pushing the waters aside, creating huge masses of splashing spray. The air was moist by the river, and cooler. Just being in proximity to the tributary brought refreshment from the dusty air of the dry terrain, which he had just traveled through. Doug wanted to drink from the river but would not. He would rather ignore his thirst, than compound his problems with the sickness Evan had warned him about.

The great river brought another disturbing thought to Doug. What if he had to cross it? The river was at least thirty yards wide and looked to be very deep and fast-moving. It would not be easy to cross at all. If he did make it to the other side, he would have to pick up the trail again, which was no sure thing as well. There were too many boulders on the far side of the river. If the creature decided to take a rock bound route, Doug would have no way of detecting the trail.

His concerns were answered by the direction of the tracks. The tributary took a lazy turn up ahead away to the left, but the tracks continued on their undeviating course, over a ridge and what looked like beyond the river valley. Doug felt a small sense of relief as he continued his hunt.

More of the day passed away. Doug marched determinedly through the underbrush following the semi-clear foot trail, but he was noticing that the brush below and the canopy were thinning out. He was getting closer to the timberline. The snow-covered peaks of the Sawtooths were coming into view. The white walls of the towering masses were in steep contrast to the branches above. The temperature had to be getting close to the freezing point. His breath was foggy now. He pulled the collar of his jacket around him. The trees were thinning out up ahead. Good. At least he would get a clear view of his surroundings. The track imprints were getting a lot more sporadic. The ground was just too hard to make any prints. Doug sensed that he was going to lose the trail again. He got to the top of a hill before he lost the trail completely. He stopped, panting heavily from the altitude change. Doug stood there and looked in all directions. Wilderness, everywhere. Not a single sign of human inhabitance. Even in the direction he had come from, there was nothing but forest, and he knew he was barely penetrating the edge of the No Return. It was a pretty place, he had to admit. Untouched and infinite. *Too bad I am going to die here,* he thought.

The loud crack of a fallen branch alerted Doug to movement not far behind him. He feared that the creature had circled back, and was ready to attack him from the rear. He turned and aimed his shotgun, waist high to face his enemy. But it was not the enemy he thought it would be.

A massive brown-colored bear stared at him from a distance of about forty feet. It stood on all fours, squarely centered on the trail he had just come from. It snorted the air in front of it, its powerful snout suspended up high, while keeping its eyes locked on Doug. The animal must have weighed over five hundred pounds. Doug took a step back, but stopped, paralyzed by the sudden memory that Evan had specifically warned him about bears. He couldn't remember the phrasing. It was escaping him. *What kind of bear is it?* It wasn't black, so it was either a grizzly or some other kind of brown bear. It had to be grizzly. It was too large to be a black bear. But what was he supposed to do? Was he supposed to stand his ground? But then, in a flash of memory, he remembered the phrase: *Grizzly, climb a tree.* Doug's course was set. Immediately, he turned and ran. The chase was on.

Doug plowed through the brush, involuntarily screaming at the top of his lungs. He scrambled as fast as he could, not daring to look back. Scanning the woods for a tree to climb, he realized that he only had one chance. He had to pick the right tree. Doug sighted a medium-sized, Lodgepole Pine not twenty feet in front of him. Nearing the tree, he dropped his shotgun and leaped in midstride for the first large branch high above him. He gained a firm handhold but the pained surged through his shoulder. Doug ignored the pain and kicked his legs to the side and wrapped them around the thick trunk near the base of the branch. He grabbed for a higher branch with one free arm, and swung his leg over the first branch. Doug could hear the bear approaching, its massive bulk barreling through the underbrush. He had to get to the second branch before the bear arrived, or it would pull him down. Every part of his body had to be high enough to escape the animal's clutches. With his last bit of energy, he put his boot onto the low branch and stepped to climb to the second tier just as the bear slammed into the trunk, almost shaking Doug from his perch. Doug's exposed back was no more than a foot above the giant carnivore.

Doug looked down at the behemoth below him. Its forepaws were leaning up against the trunk of the pine. The bear was sniffing the air once again. It dropped down on all fours and circled the tree a few times and stayed there, as if pondering its next course of action. Since it had not climbed to tree to pursue him, Doug could only assume that it was a grizzly. A black bear would have probably climbed the tree and pulled him down. He must have guessed right. Doug shifted his balance to gain a more comfortable seat on the branch. Since the shotgun was on the ground, he had no defense, so he figured he might as well get comfortable. It could be awhile.

But the grizzly seemed to have other plans. After circling the base of the tree once more, it gave a snort at Doug and continued up the trail. The giant mass of muscle lumbered up the trail, weight shifting from one hip to the other. It ambled another fifty yards or so until it was out of Doug's sight, following a clear path into the woods - the exact trail of the Bigfoot. It was then that Doug realized that he was not the intended prey after all. If the bear had a strong sense of smell, which it most assuredly did, then it would have easily caught scent of the dead Bigfoot. That's why it had not had the patience to wait for Doug to fall out of the tree. It had been after the Bigfoot all along. He thanked his luck that he had been near some climbable trees when the grizzly had caught up to him, otherwise he would have been a dead man. And by climbing the tree, and waiting it out, he must have caused the bear to lose patience and resume the hunt of its original prey.

But if he momentarily felt that luck was on his side, that quickly washed away as he considered his future course of action. What could he do now? His dilemma had just become a whole lot worse. Chasing an enraged Bigfoot through the woods was damn near impossible, but chasing a grizzly who is chasing a Bigfoot was a clear death sentence. What if the Bigfoot sensed the grizzly and pushed harder through the woods, putting more distance between itself and Doug. Or worse, what if the grizzly decided to take a break? Doug could just stumble into it without having any time to react. His odds went from impossible to worse. And he wasn't feeling any better. He felt a fever coming on, probably from the lack of food and a night spent on the river bed with a dislocated shoulder. Waves of depression were hitting him. Staying on course meant likely death, yet turning back meant life in prison, mourning the loss of his only son.

But as dismal as his options were, it wasn't much of a difficult decision. He had to continue on. He made his way cautiously down the tree and grabbed the shotgun. Doug hesitated, waiting by the trunk of the tree, fearing to leave its protection. Trees were now, he realized, his lifeline. He was going to have to move forward with greater caution, constantly assessing how close he was to a climbable tree. And he had to think that he would inevitably encounter areas where there were no trees to climb.

Mustering fortitude, he broke away from the tree and started on the trail once again. It continued, as always, along a straight line through the climbing forest. He moved as quietly as he could, guessing that the grizzly bear was not that far ahead. He had no idea how well grizzly bears could hear, but he assumed that bears could hear at least as well as humans. His guess was based on those nature shows where they would describe the incredibly acute senses of predators in the woods, where an eagle could see a mouse on a canyon floor from a mile away. Or a mountain lion could smell something from miles away. Why was it that humans had such poor senses? How did we get to the top of the food chain? Sure, we have guns now, but what did we do before we had weapons? Why didn't bears and the like just gobble us all up?

Doug continued to make his way, moving quickly from tree to tree. It was a futile effort at best. He was restricted in his pacing. Traveling too fast could result in the loss of the trail, yet going too slowly would result in the loss of the target. Making too much noise, would likely result in the loss of his life.

The pathway never strayed, but arced upwards or downwards, riding the surface of the topology. He could still hear the sounds of a raging river, not far to the north. Glades of spruce and Douglas firs rolled by, and the ground was littered with conglomerations of large gray boulders. After continuing on for another mile through an amorphous wilderness, he reached the edge of a clearing.

And there, at opposite edges of the clearing were the pieces of a puzzle that he had been chasing for days. The grizzly bear was on one side of the clearing, not fifty yards away from where Doug stood. Although he must have clearly been within range of its senses, the bear paid him no heed, for it had found its original target, that which stood on the opposite side of the clearing.

Doug quickly moved behind the visual protection of a mass of boulders before he got a good look across the way. He ducked behind the largest boulder, and placed his back against it. Fear was coursing through his veins, and he was visibly shaking, his shotgun vibrated in his trembling hands. The dark visions of the previous two nights assaulted his psyche like a whiplash. It took all of his courage to tilt his head to the side, and peek around the boulder.

Doug could see the large humanoid through a gap in the trees. It stood tall and unmoving, as if patiently waiting for the next course of action. It was the first time that Doug had seen the creature in the daylight. Overhead the sun shone down, the midday rays casting stark and short shadows across the beast. Underneath the thick coat of hair was a defined array of muscles. The creature looked powerful not just by its shear girth, but also by the rippling mass of huge muscles and sinew that covered its frame. It slowly raised its arms to the sides, with open palms towards the bear. The giant beast then lowered its center of frame, angled its back forward, raised its head and locked eyes with the grizzly. Whatever it was going to do, it did not look like it was going to retreat.

Doug noticed a small mass behind the giant being, just outside the clearing on the edge of shadow. It was propped up against a tree, a manlike shape sitting up but unmoving. It was the son. He could not see the details of the face, but he could make out the large wound on the chest of the smaller creature. It was unmistakable. A strange feeling of satisfaction came over Doug at that moment. Through all of the turmoil, he had doubted his ability to track this supposedly mythical creature, and only now did he feel that the accomplishment was close at hand.

Doug's thoughts shifted to the potential battle that seemed destined to take place. The two behemoths squared off. Who would win? Doug could not tell which animal was bigger or stronger, for they were so different in shape. The grizzly did have claws and larger teeth, but the Bigfoot was the unknown. What kind of strength did it possess? Guessing which creature would prevail, at this point, was meaningless, Doug concluded. One of them would win, and he would have to act regardless. He had to get evidence of Bigfoot's existence and get the hell out of here. The stronger animal would prevail, and he would have to kill the winner with his shotgun.

The bear started to become more agitated, pacing back and forth, yet the Bigfoot stood its ground. Doug could not help thinking that the Bigfoot was staying close to the young creature for a reason. It made sense. It must have understood that the grizzly was after the young one and not itself, for that was the scent the bear had tracked for miles through the No Return. But now the bear would have to go through the adult creature to get what it wanted.

In a great surge, the bear began a charge, and barreled at the creature. Its mass was an orchestrated turmoil of meat and fur. It rumbled at an alarming speed towards the giant humanoid. With blinding movement however, the Bigfoot crouched down, and snatched up a small boulder from the ground at its feet. There were more rocks on the ground as well, and Doug surmised that this move was not on impulse. The Bigfoot had planned this moment, and must have deliberately chosen this place to stand its ground. Up went the right arm of the creature. It leaned back, flexed its corded muscles, and threw the rock overhand towards its attacker, the missile leaving its arm at blinding speed.

The grizzly had no chance to respond. The rock crashed into its right shoulder, just missing the grizzly's head. It ripped a large gash in the bear's pelt as it careened off and ricocheted beyond the clearing. The grizzly instantly staggered back, stunned by the impact of the tremendous blow. The Bigfoot immediately repeated the tactic, launching another rock at breakneck speed towards the reeling bear. The second volley crashed into the hip of the struggling mammal. Doug could hear a loud crunching sound, as if some kind of bone had broken on the rear of the animal. The bear let out a roar of pain, but it was nowhere near done with the fight. It charged again, closing the distance between it and its formidable opponent. The Bigfoot did not have the time to arm itself once more, and decided to return the charge.

The two creatures met in a mammoth collision in the center of the clearing. A huge mass of hair and fur crashed together in a deadly embrace. The grizzly bear went up to its back two legs, its powerful jaw locking onto the flesh of the Bigfoot's left shoulder. The bear's claws began to rake against the midsection of the Bigfoot. The Bigfoot reacted by pinning its left arm against its opponents neck, while its free right arm reared back and pounded the ribs of the bear. Each creature was inflicting incredible damage to each other. If they continued, both would undoubtedly receive lethal injuries. Raining blows poured into the exposed ribcage of the grizzly, while the giant bear raked its head back and forth tearing flesh from bone. The Bigfoot decided to make the critical break by lifting its left forearm higher, and then punching inward and upward at the bear's neck. The leverage broke the bear's bite on the creature's shoulder and its head was lifted back. The bear then completely broke away, contorted its body and swung around to land on all fours again. The Bigfoot backed away towards its original position, clutching its wounded shoulder.

There was a moment of pause, as if the two combatants were assessing the situation. They could have easily battled to the death. Doug realized he must have been witnessing something no other human had ever seen. How many times had this happened before? Two giants of the wilderness battling to the end. There was no way to know. One creature was fighting for food, but the other was fighting for something different. The Bigfoot was protecting its dead son. Surely the creature knew that its offspring had died. If it was dead, why protect it so vigorously? The giant was exhibiting very unusual characteristics for an animal.

The Bigfoot then began to circle away from the bear, along the perimeter of the clearing, which was also away from the young Bigfoot body. It was a strange move, and it seemed to confuse the bear. The grizzly had been after the dead Bigfoot all along, and now the father Bigfoot opened a clear path to the young one. Maybe the creature was too mortally wounded to provide protection anymore, Doug thought. The bear charged again at a fast speed towards the adult Bigfoot, as if intending to finish it off. But then, at the last moment, it veered away and aimed for the carcass. Would the bear grab the body and drag it away, hoping that the adult Bigfoot would not give chase? No, that was not the case, for it seemed that the Bigfoot had had other intentions all along. As soon as the bear veered away from it, the Bigfoot took chase and leapt onto the great bear's back, landing on it squarely and pushing it to the ground yards short of the young lifeless Bigfoot. It must have been a feint, to draw the bear away from it to get at its backside. Now at an advantage, the great humanoid systematically positioned its huge arms underneath the grizzly's shoulders and locked them around the back of the bear's neck.

What happened next was the most frightening display of strength Doug had ever seen. The Bigfoot quickly got to its feet, all the while keeping a firm lock on the writhing bear's upper body. Then the Bigfoot let out an ungodly roar of power and began to squeeze its giant corded arms. The great sasquatch lifted the full bulk of the grizzly bear off the ground and compressed its entire upper body. Doug could hear the painful sound of flesh and cartilage being torn from bone. The bear let out a painful whine as the Bigfoot's arms fully extended and snapped both arms of the bear away from their sockets and back into an awkward position. The bear went limp instantly, in shock from the immense trauma. It was dropped to the ground in an immobile heap, its spine shattered in the process. The Bigfoot then staggered away, found a large boulder, lifted it high over its head, and sent it crashing down on the grizzly's large head, crushing its skull. The bear was dead. The battle was over.

Doug turned back from the scene and took in a deep breath, realizing that he had not taken a breath in the past minute from the adrenaline rush. The Bigfoot's power was unbelievable. If Chad had taken an ounce of the beating that bear had just taken, there was no way he could still be alive. The thought was both depressing and paralyzing, and Doug could not shake the feeling that all of his efforts were in vain. But, he had to shoot the creature now, while it was within close range. He had one shot, and no other reason for being here, so he had to act now. Mustering up what courage he had left, he took another deep breath and slowly turned to put the creature in his sights.

The creature was still there, but looking right at Doug. It was standing between him and the dead grizzly, already closing the distance. It must have sensed him, possibly even before the fight had started. When it made eye contact with Doug, it snarled and let out a roar. A prickly sensation shot up Doug's neck, overwhelmed, as he was, by raw fear. He had the creature in his sights, but the shotgun was wavering all over the place in his shaking hands. The Bigfoot charged him at full speed. The image danced in and out of the target scope. Doug was torn. He could take the chance and fire, but if he missed, it would be all over. He could not shake what the Bigfoot had just done to the grizzly. Fear got the better of him. He leapt to his feet and started to run.

Doug ran away as fast as he could. He screamed, yelling "Help me?!" into the woods as he ran on. His plea was useless. The Bigfoot gave relentless chase. Doug could hear the rolling mass of broken branches behind him. It was twenty yards behind him, now. The creature was gaining. There were no trees to climb. It didn't matter because Doug thought that the Bigfoot could climb trees. *The Bigfoot could probably do anything a man could do,* he thought. *There's no escape. I'll be ripped apart.* Although Doug felt that there was no hope, he had to think about using the shotgun. When the Bigfoot closed on him, he could turn and fire. But the anxiety was too much, he knew. It would require extreme coordination to stop, turn, and accurately take aim on the charging beast. And Doug could not coordinate his efforts now. He knew that he would miss, and the creature would be upon him. He ran on as the sounds behind him grew louder. The giant humanoid was gaining ground on him at every step.

Doug then heard a different sound. It was a sound up ahead, in the direction he was running. The sound was coming from everywhere now, a low murmur turning into a turbulent noise. It was the sound of rushing water. He was coming close to the rapids of a river. He could see the woods clearing up ahead. Doug rushed on, his lungs starting to burn. The clearing was coming close, and the Bigfoot roared behind him. The sasquatch was not ten yards away from him now, and gaining fast. He dashed into the open area, but could not see the river. The land appeared to end at a shear drop. He knew that he must have been high above the rushing waters. He made a split second decision, and threw the shotgun into the brush at the side of the clearing. If he had leapt into the waters with the shotgun, it might not have fired again. It was his only weapon, and if he lost it, he would have no protection, if he lived. As Doug reached the rocky ledge of the clearing, he jumped high and far into the air, and looked down to see his fate.

The raging waters were below him, not thirty feet below, but they did not look very deep. Doug plummeted down and crashed into four feet of white water and grazed a large rock with his right hip, careening his body off to the left. The clean rock tore a gash through his pants. Doug rebounded into white water with a loud splash. The fast waters instantly took him away, undulating up and down over the rocks. He fought desperately to right himself so that he could breathe amidst the splashing torrent. The pain was severe. He bobbed and rolled onto his back and looked back to see the giant humanoid standing at the ledge that he had just leapt from. The creature just stood there as Doug pulled away, the current bullying him downstream.

Darrell, Evan and T-Bone made much better progress in the daylight. T-Bone was following the trail easily enough, and they had a pretty good feeling that she was on the right track, judging by her continued lack of enthusiasm. Every once in a while, they would scrutinize the ground for tracks, and resume.

"Good dog." Evan repeatedly assured her, letting her know she was doing the right thing. He was amazed that this dog, who had never been scared of anything, including bear, would be scared of this animal. He doubted that she had ever caught a whiff of a Bigfoot before, so she must be instinctively afraid of them. She kept stopping and looking back, as if to say: *Do I have to track this thing?*

Darrell tried to communicate repeatedly with Forsythe, but to no avail. Darrell could only think of two possibilities as to why the CB wasn't working. Either the batteries were dying, which he had no way of testing or fixing. Or, these mountains just simply didn't like radio waves, which he had no way of avoiding. Either way, Darrell and Evan had lost communication access to any kind of aid they might need. The fact was that they were ill-equipped for a rescue mission. They had no first-aid kit and no fresh water. They had gone far too deep into the forest to be able to carry someone out who was in need of urgent medical attention. It would take several days to carry a body through this terrain, all the way to the campsite. And without the CB working, they would not be able to call a rescue chopper. The only people that were getting out of this forest would be those that could move on their own accord.

At noon they reached the riverbed where Doug had been attacked the night before. It wasn't long before T-Bone found the blood on the rocks, both the young Bigfoot's and Doug's, in the area where he had landed on his head. T-Bone circled around the area as if there were many places where footfalls had occurred.

"I'm guessing this is where the shotgun blasts and howls came from last night." Darrell concluded and Evan agreed. "There's quite a bit of blood here. I hope it's not Doug's."

"Well, we heard a number of gun blasts. Maybe Doug killed it." Evan added.

"Do you think we might have missed him if he was heading back?"

"Well ... it's possible. But I honestly don't think so. The forest is pretty wide but I am assuming that Doug is trying to remember the way he came so that he doesn't get lost. He might have gone back down the trail when we diverted, but I think T-Bone would have picked that up. So far it has been a one-way trip."

"Yeah, and I don't think he would hide from us if he had the kill. I'm assuming a lot here but I would think he would seek us out, once he had his evidence. When we were interrogating Doug back in Omah, it really felt like he was hiding something. I had no idea what he would be hiding at the time, but now it makes complete sense. Bigfoot docs not make for the best of alibis if you don't have any evidence." Darrell had trailed off as he noticed something. "Hey take a look at this!" He gestured toward the pathway of destruction from the Bigfoot rush.

"Jesus." Evan gasped as he came up to the edge of the forest to look. "That's amazing. Look at that." Evan looked back at the blood. "You said that the animal that you saw when you were a kid was eating the elk right?"

"Yeah." Darrell responded.

"Well you don't think that it would eat a human, do you?"

"I don't think so. They must have territorial diets just like any other animal, which I sincerely doubt includes humans."

"Why do you say that?" Evan asked.

"Because I think we would have heard a lot more about Bigfoot if they ate humans." Darrell concluded. "More historical accounts of attacks or news reports of missing people or something to that effect. But there's nothing like that, ... that I know of."

"Yeah, you're probably right." Evan relented.

"Hey, I've got a question for you." Darrell asked. "Let's assume that Doug has wounded the thing. The blood we found back at the blind had to have been from something other than Doug and Chad, because they did not have any blood, or open wounds, on them when I found them on the highway. Maybe the blood is from a later time, after Doug escaped from jail, but let's assume that its not. Let's assume the blood was spilled before I found them."

"Ok, I got you so far, but what was the question?" Evan asked.

"I'm getting to it. Now, we find blood here at the riverbed. This could be Doug's blood, and by the sounds from last night, it is highly possible that Doug got hurt. But again, let's assume this is Bigfoot blood. So, in theory, Doug hit the creature twice, once back at the camp and once here. Now the tracks have basically been in a straight line from the camp to here, or so it seems. They definitely haven't been meandering. My question is: Is that kind of behavior normal for a wounded animal? Or better yet, is that kind of behavior normal for a top of the food chain animal, which I am assuming this thing is?"

"Good question. I don't know. It's kind of odd. I wounded a bear once, and it took me five hours to find it after shooting it. It had crawled right into this high bramble area. What I do know is that when a top predator has no natural enemies, they pretty much die of old age like us humans. When they know that they are going to die, they go hide, if you will, whether it be in a cave or in some bushes. I know that sounds weird because, well, where do you hide if you're a big animal that already lives in the woods? But that's the way it is. That's why you never see dead bear carcasses. No one has. Ever."

"Ever?"

"Only on the side of the road, if they were hit by a car... but never a natural causes bear." said Evan.

"That's very interesting. So do you think this thing is going to its cave or something?"

"I don't know. An animal wouldn't have traveled this far if it had gotten shot. We must have gone ten miles already. It's definitely weird. This creature must have a lot of territory."

Something clicked in Darrell's mind. "Or maybe it's nomadic. My father told me that these animals would appear at random, in long intervals, even years. My tribe knew the surrounding wilderness and all the animals within it, even the Yeahoh, the Giant Ones, which is what we called them. They were also known as the great visitors, for they never stayed for long. Always on the move. When our land got slowly squeezed by civilization, the elders believed that the Yeahoh had just moved on, but did not die out. My sighting was the last time anybody saw one in my tribe, and that was over twenty-five years ago." Darrell stated.

"So you think they travel all over?"

"They must and must have for a long time. The Nez Perce definitely saw them here, probably pretty frequently."

"Why do you say that?" Evan asked.

"Because the Nez Perce word for Bigfoot is Omah. And for some reason, I don't think the word would have become the name of the area for no reason."

"Shit. I have been living in this town for twenty years, and I didn't know that it was named after Bigfoot."

"There are a few places like that, that I know of anyway, like Skookum Meadows up in Washington, and Windego, Minnesota. They are all named after the Giant One. Just no one remembers because the people that named them are all gone."

"Where did the people go?" Evan wished he hadn't have asked that, right after it came out of his mouth. He was pretty sure he knew the answer.

Darrell stopped, "They were relocated or killed."

"Right." Evan apologized, "Sorry."

"It's OK Evan, it's not your fault. The genocide of the Native American peoples took place a long time before you were born. And no one is asking for an apology, just awareness."

Evan couldn't help but feel a little awkward. He prided himself on being impartial to the Indians and their history, but it was obvious to him how little he knew about their culture.

Darrell spoke again. "Another thing about the Nez Perce was that they didn't hang around here too much. This place was definitely within their territory, but they stayed away from the No Return. Most of their settlements were farther to the north, along the northern tributaries of the Salmon River. The Shoshone might have come up from the plains in the south to hunt, but we are pretty far from their main territories."

"Do you think the Nez Perce were afraid of this place?" Evan asked.

"Don't know. It could have been just that there was better game where they lived, so there was no incentive to come here."

"Well, I don't know, maybe the situation has changed

in the last couple hundred years, but I can tell you that the hunting here is damn good." Evan conceded.

"Which reminds me that I need to talk to you about that? You are aware of gaming rules within protected wildlife refuges, right?" Darrell questioned him.

"Don't worry, once we find Doug, I am never coming back here ever again to hunt, or for anything else, ever."

Darrell smiled. "I believe you. Don't worry Evan. I wasn't going to do anything. I was just giving you shit."

T-Bone had picked up the scent on the other side of the stream. They traveled up the bed until they reached the same embankment that Doug had scurried up after the Bigfoot. Up higher, in the softer mud, shoe prints and giant footprint tracks were visible. Two things could be determined from the climb. One was that both Doug and the animal were still alive, and the other was that they were continuing to head east, farther into the No Return.

Doug swirled around in the water for minutes, letting the current take him into slower waters before swimming to one side of the river. With his one good arm and one good leg, he paddled up to a soft beach and collapsed on the shore. He was still alive. The gash on his leg was bleeding freely, but did not look

life threatening. He got to his feet to see if he could put
weight on his leg. The pain was severe but not
overwhelming, and he found that he could stand. He
must not have broken any bones. He felt that luck
was with him again.

He ambled up the high cliff bank and made his way
back up the side of the river to retrieve his shotgun.
The Bigfoot could have been anywhere and attacked
him at any time, he knew, but what choice did he
have? He had to get the shotgun quickly before he lost
more time and distance to the creature. Hopefully, he
could go to the clearing and retrieve the dead Bigfoot.

The bank slowly rose until it was about thirty feet
above the water line. The rapids below increased in
energy and speed as he came to the recognizable
narrows where he had made his leap. He walked into
the clearing, fearing the Bigfoot would still be standing
there, but the animal was nowhere to be found. He
quickly ran over to the other edge of the clearing and
searched the bushes for his shotgun. It was easy to
find, resting upon a thorn bush. He picked it up and
examined it, noting that it did not look damaged.

He made his way back to the clearing where he had
hoped to find the dead Bigfoot. Doug wondered if he
would ever have a better shot at killing the giant
Bigfoot again. Not thirty minutes ago, the creature
had been plainly in his gun sight, at close range in
broad daylight. The chance at a shot couldn't get
much better than that. But he had panicked and could
not fire the weapon. He could have shot the creature

point-blank in the face when it was right on top of him, but he could not overcome his fear. He told himself that he would not squander his next chance, if he had one.

Doug arrived at the clearing and his hopes slipped away again. The giant bear carcass sat right in the middle of the clearing, flies already circling about it, but the dead Bigfoot was gone. He walked to where the Bigfoot body once was and peered at the depression in the grass. In spite of the pain, fatigue and starvation stretching over days, he had not gotten any further towards his goal. In fact, he was worse off now than he was before. He had only one shotgun shell left, and he was badly injured in his shoulder and hip. He was running out of energy. But worst of all, he knew, was that the element of surprise was gone. There was no way that the Bigfoot would give up the baby Bigfoot without a fight. He looked back instinctively at the bear carcass. The grizzly bear was recognized as the greatest predator on this continent, and yet it had been ripped apart by this creature. What chance did *he* really have? The Bigfoot was truly a legendary beast. Doug recalled the look in its eyes when it had stared at him as he tumbled down the rapids. Its expression was a strange one, not of a frustrated predator whose prey had escaped. Its eyes and face seemed calm and resolute. Doug did not understand the significance. He could not put it all together. But there was something nagging at him, something that made it fit, but he was not sure why. He pondered the creature's behavior while he found the foot trail once again and set his course for deeper into the wild.

Pete Travers

CHAPTER TWELVE

Doug followed the familiar straight-line course through the climbing terrain. He paused and looked at the mountains that were opening up before him. The jagged line continued in a north-south direction as far as the eye could see. The name of the range had obvious origins. The Sawtooth Mountains, an extension of the Rockies, were a part of a very young range by geological standards, so they were quite sharp compared to the rolling hill nature of the older ranges, like the Appalachians. Carved by glaciers, the giant ice juggernauts ripped through the terrain as the crustal plates thrust the land higher every day, creating one the harshest of landscapes. Each one of the Sawtooth peaks was shaped like a shark's tooth with a sharp triangular point at the top. In the area Doug was heading, due east by the sun, there was a pass in the range, where two mountains met at about two thousand feet below their respective summits.

Suddenly, he saw it. Movement on the mountain face,

a mile away, on the edge of the pass, a tiny dark shape moving on a sea of white. He would never have noticed it, were it not for the snow-covered, contrasted backdrop. He pulled up the gun to look through the scope. The magnification showed a dark manlike shape, its legs pumping up the incline at a steady pace. Draped over one shoulder was a smaller dark shape. The creature had the baby Bigfoot with him. Even with the weight of the young one, it was still moving remarkably fast. Doug watched for a few minutes through the gun sight, as his distant target crossed over the pass and disappeared. The display of speed and power exhibited by the creature reminded Doug of how futile his chances were in catching up to and disabling the beast.

Doug made a mental note of where the Bigfoot had crossed over the ridge, memorizing the rock shapes peeking through the snow. He could see a distinct V-shaped rock near the very top of the pass. He knew he had to get to that point regardless of the path he chose, so there was no use in spending effort trying to find the trail. At least he could move faster for the next few miles. *As fast as one could go climbing up a big mountain,* Doug corrected himself. He trudged forward at a light jog. He couldn't move too fast because of the pain in his shoulder, hip and back. Doug focused on the ground in front of him, one step at a time.

Things weren't going well for the search party. Clouds

were rolling in fast from the west and moisture was
starting to drop from the sky. The dogs were having
trouble picking up the scent, and tracks were being
washed away. Forsythe was still trying to
communicate with Darrell, but without luck.

Forsythe wanted to get his hands on Childress. It
seemed clear to him that Childress was going to great
lengths to evade the law, hiding deep in the No Return.
He had seen stronger reactions to an arrest before,
and Childress had gone into the jail without a fight.
The young deputy theorized that Childress didn't resist
because he *knew* he could break out. Childress might
have had an accomplice. The jailbreak was clean, with
no signs of forced exit. The cell door had been
unlocked or picked, but not broken open. The only
plausible scenario was that the lock had been picked
from the outside, with the right type of tools. Forsythe
wondered for a moment if Evan Radcliffe, a carpenter,
had been an accomplice all along. Radcliffe could have
helped Childress escape and returned home to wait for
the sheriff to call on him for questioning. Then
Radcliffe would take the sheriff on a wild goose chase
into the local forest, while Childress was on his way to
Canada. It made sense to Forsythe, and if his theory
was true, then the sheriff was alone in a potentially
dangerous situation. It was all the more reason to
keep moving.

Forsythe questioned the sheriff's judgment on bringing
an assailant's best friend on a two-man search party
into the wilderness. *I would never have done that,*
Forsythe thought. He wondered if he should increase

the manpower of the search party. There was such a consistent canopy of trees out here that a helicopter search would prove useless, especially in this kind of lousy weather. And with no fire roads this deep into the No Return, tracking on foot was their only option. The deputy determined that moving forward with his current search party was the best that he could do.

Since the scent was lost, Forsythe told the group to fan out, in the hopes of covering more ground to possibly pick up the scent once more. They continued on in the direction that the scent seem to be heading, but the rain was relentless, rendering the dogs useless.

They trudged along as best they could, but Forsythe knew that any chance of catching Childress, if he was out here, was probably with the sheriff. Eventually, Childress would either be caught, or die out in the wilderness. Either way, it would bring satisfaction to Forsythe.

Doug's progress was just as impeded. The snow was getting deeper as the slope of the terrain increased. He was about halfway up the mountain pass, about a half-mile from the top. His thighs were burning from the ascent, but he was determined to keep going. As he pulled in the dry air, he was reminded of how thirsty he was. He looked down at the white covered earth. He debated for a moment on whether the snow was safe to eat. Weighing his options, he grabbed a pile of it and fed it slowly into his mouth. It was ice cold, but still refreshing to his body, which had not received water more than a day. If he were to get a disease from it, so be it, Doug thought. It was the least of his problems.

The solitude was getting to Doug. He was starting to talk to himself, falling into hallucinatory conversations with others. He thought of his wife.

There was so much anger. He did not want the anger anymore. He remembered her face. It was the same face he had looked at for so many years. There had been complete trust. Doug always knew that Ellen would never have cheated on him. Maybe it was a gender thing, but Doug felt like Ellen knew exactly what made her happy. He wasn't very romantic with her, not as often as he should have been. Whenever he was ready, she was always ready. She was the one who cleaned up, lit the candles. Ellen was always the one who drove the spiritual side of their relationship. They were not religious, but Ellen was the one who provoked their conversations about life and death. He had taken it for granted. He wanted it back. He wanted to go back in time, before they were divorced, before he had slept with Chloe.

Chloe had worked at the bank. She was a teller, transferred from Seattle by choice. She had wanted to get out of the city, and go someplace else. Omah was definitely someplace else. They had an attraction to each other the moment they met. It was a harmless flirtation at first, but it became more serious as time went on. He felt the guilt in the beginning, but tried to remind himself that he wasn't doing anything wrong.

The trouble started when he grew tired of going home. Doug compared Ellen to Chloe. Chloe represented fun and freedom. Ellen represented responsibility. He grew detached from his wife. He stayed close to Chad, but Ellen drifted away from his thoughts. She wanted to reach out to him but could not figure out how, and became increasingly frustrated. He stayed more at work. Chloe seemed to stay late at work as well. Ellen clearly noticed the change and asked why work was so busy. *"Who else has to work late?"* she would ask. He would lie and say only himself. Off he went to work without looking into her eyes.

The divorce happened quickly. There was never a fight. No true feelings were spilled out. Somehow, Ellen had found out about the affair, but Doug never had the courage to ask how. One day as he was about to stroll off to work, Ellen told him she wanted a divorce. Chloe had left the bank a month earlier and moved to the East coast, the physical part of the affair only lasting about a week. Doug didn't know what to do. He just let the whole thing bowl over him. When Ellen used the domestic violence accusation in the divorce court, he didn't fight it. He just sat quiet and took his medicine. The damage was done and it was irreparable. Now he was alone. Now he was alone and in a world of shit, Doug corrected himself. He was so tired.

Back in the lower elevations, Darrell and Evan noticed a distinct change in T-Bone. Her excitement picked up considerably as she tugged at her leash, wanting to run down the trail. Evan took notice and bent to the ground to check the tracks for any clues to her behavior. His reaction was immediate.

"Whoa." Evan uttered.

"What?" the sheriff asked.

"Things just got a lot worse." Evan replied.

Darrell leaned over to look at the tracks that Evan was bent over. The tracks of the Bigfoot and Doug were now matched by a third animal whose claws marks were unmistakable.

"Bear." Darrell concluded.

"Worse. Grizzly bear." Evan added.

"Really? In these woods?" Darrell remarked. "I thought that the grizzly bear only ventured in Glacier National Park in Montana and Canada."

"Not true. It's rare, but I think that they wander down deep into Idaho during the spring months. They come here for the salmon. I've seen sign of them here a few times."

"So do you think the bear is after Doug?" Darrell asked.

Evan lifted his hat and scratched his sweaty mop of hair, wincing and closing his eyes to try to think clearly. He shook his head in befuddlement. "I don't know. Grizzly bear do not hunt down humans for food, unless they have already had a taste for human. And if there is a grizzly bear that has already done that, they are usually found and put down. For a bear to come this far down into Idaho, I would think that it would have caused a mess farther north that we would have heard about on the news."

"I haven't heard anything to that effect on the police ban." Darrell added.

"Yeah, something tells me that bear is after the Bigfoot, but that doesn't make things any better." Evan concluded.

"Because Doug is right in the middle." Darrell finished the train of thought.

"Damn." Evan was demoralized. He could not think that Doug's chances of surviving were that good at all. "It's my fault. If I hadn't convinced Doug to go hunting, he wouldn't be in danger. Fuck." Evan threw his hat down in anger.

"It's no one's fault, Evan. Did you suspect Bigfoot would be out here? It's pointless to feel guilty about something out of your control." Darrell grabbed the dog leash out of Evan's hands and let T-Bone drive him farther up the trail. "Let's move Evan. We are not going to help Doug by standing here."

Evan reined in on his building anger and followed Darrell. He knew that the sheriff was right.

They moved quickly after that, with the bloodhound driving at a good speed through the foothills. Her anxiety was clearly heightening. She was getting close to her target and reacting as she had before. They were reminded of what else had happened before, how they had lost precious ground when the dog derailed their efforts by following the scent of a turkey. At this speed, they could only have faith that T-Bone was on the right trail. It seemed a necessary risk, considering the potential danger to Doug if they did not catch up to him in time.

After a mile, they arrived at the clearing where the battle had taken place just a few hours before. They were shocked by the sight before them. The huge carcass of the grizzly lay on its stomach in the center of the clearing with its dislocated arms spread out to the sides. A large pool of blood spread around the smashed head.

"My God." Darrell gasped. He let go of the dog leash as T-Bone cautiously entered the clearing and circled the dead beast. Both men leveled their shotguns to a ready position. They were speechless. The raw power of what it would take to bring down a beast like this was unfathomable. The animal was not killed by a piercing wound, rather it was destroyed by brute force and broken.

It was ironic that Evan had just explained that no one had ever seen a dead bear in the woods and yet here they were, gazing upon a master predator, killed by another species. And it wasn't by luck either. The battle appeared to have been decisive. The confusion lie in what had happened to Doug. Darrell located tracks on the ground and tried to put the puzzle together.

"Doug must have been following behind the bear, because I can see his tracks around the kill. He must have either witnessed what happened here or came upon it sometime thereafter." Darrell concluded.

Evan took T-Bone's leash and persuaded the dog, as best he could, to find any sign of what had left the clearing. T-Bone circled the kill wider and wider until she came upon the depression in the grass at the edge of the clearing where the dead Bigfoot once lay. T-Bone resorted back to her timid behavior and Evan knew that this marked their new scent to track. Evan could also see boot tracks in the soft earth, which confirmed that Doug was still ahead of them. He wished that Doug would stop and give up, and all would be fine, but that was not to be the case.

Doug wanted to stop, but one thing kept him moving: the huge footprints in the snow. He had picked up the tracks near the snowline, about a half-mile down from where he now walked. One step at a time, he pushed himself through the pain. There was no way he could match the creature's stride, step for step, but he fell into an even rhythm of exactly half the stride, his feet falling into a giant print every other time. The shotgun was held in his freezing hands as balance. Every time he regained full consciousness from his drunken-like state, he was suddenly aware of the hopelessness of his situation. Slowly, he would fall back into a hypnotic rhythm. *Keep moving. Almost at the top,* Doug urged himself. He trudged on for another hour.

And then, out of his peripheral vision, in the bright blinding snow, Doug could see a large dark shape looming not five feet in front of him. He leapt backwards from sheer instinct, screaming while holding his shotgun at both ends like a stick in defense. He fell into the snow and slid away some twenty feet down the face of the mountain, making a micro-avalanche as the disturbed snow came down after him. The turbulent slide painfully reminded him of his recent injuries, and added to the effect as his shoulder hit an unforgiving boulder buried in the snow.

Doug looked up into the blinding incline. The dark shape was standing very still. As a matter of fact it was not moving at all. It was a rock. *Jesus Christ! I got scared by a fucking rock!* He could see it more clearly as his eyes adjusted. Other rocks like it littered the surrounding hillside, peeking through the blanket of white snow. Something clicked in his mind. Doug scanned the immediate area of formations and noticed the recognizable V-shaped boulder less than one hundred yards up the mountain. He was at the top. Energy returning, he rolled over and climbed to his feet, and started to make his way up the mountain again. He trudged up to the top, not knowing what lay on the other side. He had never gone this far into a wilderness and had certainly never hiked at this elevation. Doug climbed the last steps leading to the top, still following the giant's trail. He peeked out over the edge to look at the other side, not knowing what to expect.

The view was both beautiful and devastating to the man's emotions. Pure vastness. Doug was so high he could see the curvature of the earth. Mountains knifing through the endless landscapes past the horizon. Their snowcapped peaks, like the whitest of teeth, biting through the terrain below. Now he knew why they called it the No Return. He was not going back. It looked like something out of a dream, a land that only nature touched and only nature witnessed. Just looking at it made him feel like he was not welcome here. Doug dropped to his knees. The logical part of his brain was trying to tell himself that this is what he should have expected, but something in him had been hoping for an easy way out. Tears fell from his eyes. Never in all of his guesses did he imagine he would die like this, out in the wilderness, alone, starving, freezing. Doug dropped to his side, rolled onto his back and stared into the sky. He could feel his limbs getting numb. Overcome with fatigue, Doug figured he could just fall asleep here and never wake up. His eyes closed, and he felt the coldness overtake him.

CHAPTER THIRTEEN

Darrell and Evan arrived at the timberline, less than two hours behind Doug. The cold view ahead gave them little comfort, as the towering white rock masses climbed into the sky. The two men and the dog had made good time, mostly because they were aware of the storm clouds behind them and knew what it would mean for Doug if they were to lose the trail in the rain. The jogging was wearing them down as well. They had not eaten for a while and they had almost as little sleep as Doug. Evan urged for a break. The altitude was making their lungs burn for air, so they stopped to catch their breath.

Darrell was gasping. "Well I'd say we are gaining ground, but that's only a guess."

Evan responded through breaths. "Yeah ... I ... think we may be ... heading into those mountains." He gestured towards the higher elevation peaks.

"And those clouds are catching up to us. I do not want to get caught up there in a snowstorm. That could get real dangerous."

"Yeah." Evan responded, at a loss.

"Yeah is right...What to do?" Darrell said, hitting a mental wall. He reasoned that they were probably closer to Doug than they had been in a while. If only they could get him to slow down.

"What do you think Doug would do if he knew someone was out here?"

"It depends...I guess."

"If he thought it was a search party, he'd probably still run. We have to assume that he thinks, we think, he hurt Chad." It hurt just sorting that through. "If he thought it was a hunter, maybe he would think to illicit the help of someone."

"Maybe. Who knows what mental condition he's in? I gotta tell ya, Darrell," he paused to catch another breath, "... knowing Doug, it's pretty fuckin' amazing that he's gotten this far. He's never been hunting before, and he's not even really the outdoorsy type. The guy's a banker for Christ's sake."

"But he's got some real motivation right now. So, the question is, do we let him know that we are here?" Darrell asked.

"I don't know. I mean, I guess you could say I'm his best friend..." Evan thought that it was funny that this was the first time he had ever said *best friend* concerning Doug or had even really thought about it, "...but I really don't know how he would react to our presence. Doug's a really normal guy, but he's never been in this kind of situation before, but, shit, who fucking has? I don't have a goddamn clue."

Darrell responded. "OK, well, the way I'm thinking is that we don't have much to lose right now because at the pace he's going, I don't think we are going to catch up to him before he heads over the range. And if we lose his trail on the other side, he's pretty much on his own regardless, because no one is going to find him in there once this rain goes through." He could tell that moisture was going to fall soon.

Evan agreed. They had nothing to lose. Evan and Darrell raised their shotguns and fired repeated blasts into the sky.

Doug awoke groggily to the shotgun blasts. They seemed far away, but he could hear them distinctly enough to wake from his sleep. His body was lying fully in the snow and was starting to feel numb. He lay there, staring at the bright sky. Consciousness and his immediate history were slowly returning.

Somebody is out here.

He sat up and looked about. The sounds definitely came from the direction he had traveled. Was someone following him? Was it a search party? They sounded miles away, so they must have tracked him down at least to the base of the mountains. But why would they be shooting? What are they shooting at if they are a search party? The blasts sounded too far away to be aimed at him. It may be hunters, which would explain the gunfire. The odd thing was that the shots were occurring at regular intervals, as if they were not shooting *at* anything. There were just repeated blasts, every second or so. Doug surmised that it was probably a search party, and they were probably signaling to another party that they had found his trail, and that they were close.

Well here it is, they are after me, Doug thought. *They are going to hunt me down.* He could only assume that Chad was dead now. He just didn't think they had manhunts for child abusers, so Chad must have passed away. Now it's murder. The concept of Doug being tried for murder mattered very little to him now. His future seemed so trivial compared to the emotional weight of Chad's death on his mind. *Why couldn't I have taken Chad to a football game or something?* Doug asked himself. He couldn't get the vision of Chad being attacked by that creature out of his mind. Chad's last conscious moments must have been horrifying. He was crying again. Doug wanted to die.

His thoughts moved towards his current predicament. There was no way he would let them capture him alive.

*I'll just keep marching into these woods and they'll
never find me.* He looked at the expanse around him
and the valley below him. Thank God the shotguns
had awakened him. Otherwise, his pursuers would
have caught up to him, snoozing on top of the
mountain range. Not anymore. Adrenaline got him to
his feet. He looked at how the Bigfoot tracks knifed
their way through the ravine down into the forested
valley below. At the center of the valley was a river,
cutting through the trees. He trudged forward, more of
a constant fall than anything as he half-slid down the
mountainside to the valley below. He had an
overpowering sensation about this place that he was
going to die here, one way or another. Nevertheless,
he continued on, caring little for his own safety.

Forsythe's search party was still having terrible luck.
The rain was pouring down now a few miles east of the
Sawtooth range. Their pace was getting slower and
slower and the men knew that the trail was only going
to get colder by the minute. The dogs were wandering
about, obviously distracted and practically useless due
to the lack of scent. Forsythe tried the radio, but there
was still nothing. He spat at the ground. This was
starting to look hopeless, he thought. Forsythe
wanted to help in the capture of Childress, but he
feared that his search party would be rendered
ineffective. If their luck did not change considerably in
the next couple of hours, they would have to rethink
the search and possibly switch to helicopters, which
was a long shot option at best. Helicopters could cover

a lot more ground, but would be useless if the hunted did not want to be caught. It was too easy to hide in the dense forest. He wondered if Childress would give himself up. He couldn't be sure, for Childress had already surprised him by escaping from jail and fleeing into the wilderness. *Where did the asshole think he was going?* Forsythe wondered. The No Return was one the dumbest of places to hide if you planned on living for more than a week. It would take ten times that amount of time, just to hike across it. Forsythe could only determine two possibilities to Childress's actions: one, that Childress was out of his mind and was not long for this world, or two, that he was going somewhere into the wilderness, someplace specific. Forsythe pondered that thought as the rain poured down on his search party.

Darrell and Evan were having only slightly better luck. It was becoming clear that it would be difficult to stay ahead of the snow. They had to move fast because if enough snow fell, it would cover the prints and the trail would be lost. Tiny flakes started to fall around them. The clouds above them had crashed into the mountains, and very soon, Darrell and Evan would be climbing through them. The cloud cover had also blocked much of the light from the waning sun.

"Darrell, ...where do you ... think we are going?" Evan pushed out through labored gasps.

"Straight." Darrell muttered.

"What?" Evan stopped and turned. "Did you say straight?"

"Yeah, have you noticed?" Darrell asked.

"Yes! I have. We go up and down the terrain, but we are not making any turns. Doug's been going in a straight line for miles." Evan concluded.

"Actually, he's been following something else that has been going in a straight line for miles." Darrell corrected.

"Right. What the fuck would a Bigfoot walk in a straight line for? It seems kind of stupid if it wants to get away from Doug."

"I don't think that it is so much that it's trying to get away from Doug, rather that it's going somewhere specific."

"What do you mean?" Evan asked.

The sheriff shrugged. "Who knows? Maybe a hiding place or something."

Evan looked up the mountain at that notion. The wide snow trail followed straight up the mountain and out of the visible range of the flashlight. On the trail, Evan could easily see the tracks of Doug's boots, outlined by the huge impression of a bare five-toed giant. The size differential between the two tracks was unmistakable.

Doug, what the fuck are you doing? Evan thought.

The nagging point in Evan's mind voiced itself. "I don't understand."

"What?" Darrell asked.

"What is it?" Evan returned back.

"What is what?" Darrell replied but he thought he understood.

"What is Bigfoot? What are we after? What is it? Is it a primate? Is it part man?" Evan barraged Darrell with questions between labored breaths.

"No one knows." Darrell shrugged.

"What do you think it is?" Evan asked.

"You don't want to know."

"Yes I do. Tell me."

Darrell stopped to catch his breath, and Evan stopped for a break as well. They were standing in the plowed snow trail of the giant beast. At this altitude, it was impossible to speak for a prolonged period of time. "Well, after seeing a Bigfoot, one becomes unavoidably curious about their existence. I mean, it changes things, in a big way. For one, we are not the only beings walking around on two feet anymore. Something else is out there. Something that must be closely related to us. For most people who have seen television shows on Bigfoot, I bet it all seems like entertainment. But for me, I knew it was real, and I knew some of the information on those shows could be taken as truthful."

"Like what?" Evan asked.

"Like where the sightings occurred. Sure, people could be lying about what they saw, but I bet a lot of the sightings are based in truth. There's a lot of wilderness out here. There are literally thousands of square miles in this country where something big could hide. Not to mention Canada. And there's quite a bit of evidence, albeit circumstantial, that indicates that they roam all over North America. The stuff that's really odd is the DNA samples."

"DNA? How the hell did we get DNA from a Bigfoot if we can't get a picture of one?" Evan doubted.

"Hair. They will collect hair from areas where sightings occurred. The hair will snag on a bush or something."

"How do they know that it's not human hair?" Evan asked.

"They don't. The stuff they tested was too close to call, but I have a feeling why. Do you know how close genetically a human is to our closest relative, the chimpanzee?" Darrell asked.

"I don't know." Evan shrugged.

"Ninety-eight percent. Horses and zebras are more genetically different than we are to chimps."

"Whoa, so what about the Bigfoot hairs?"

"Well the DNA specialists that examined the hairs, cither were reluctant to publish their findings or they stated that the hairs were probably human. The reason being that the hairs were too close to human code to be anything but human."

"What do you mean 'too close'?"

"Well, different people have slightly different DNA from each other, otherwise we would all be identical to a certain degree. So there's a differential between all people of the world, a range that we all fall in, to be human that is. The range is about one half of one percent of the total genetic code." The sheriff stated.

"I got ya, ... so far."

"Well, most of the supposed Bigfoot hairs that they found fell just outside of that range, about point two percent outside the lines. It was too close to call. No scientist in their right mind was going to say that this was proof of a Bigfoot."

"So do you think that Bigfoot is our ancestor or something?"

"Either that or we're its." Darrell looked Evan in the

eyes.

Evan paused and his eyes went wide. "Whoa. What?"

"Why not? My people migrated over from Asia across the Alaskan ice bridge many thousands of years ago, along with the rest of the primates that settled here and in Central America. We evolved from homo erectus, which came from China. Why couldn't we have evolved into something new?"

"But why would we go backwards?"

"What do you mean by backwards? Getting bigger and stronger. Developing thicker hair to live out in the cold harsher climates. Heightened senses to see at night or smell at great distances. Evolution wise, it seems like the way to go to live here. You wouldn't last a week out in these woods without any means to sustain yourself, other than nature around you. Doug better..." The sheriff trailed off as he realized he was moving onto awkward ground. "We better get moving." He concluded.

Evan was left with more confusing thoughts. The two climbed on.

Doug continued down into the valley. The tree line came upon him. Once he was in tree cover, things got a lot darker. The snow cover on the ground gave way to mossy vegetation and wet earth. It was very late afternoon, and the sun, already low, would soon be setting in the west behind him, behind the mountains.

If he had not been paying closer attention to his surroundings, he would not have noticed it.

Carved right out of a very old tree stump, was what looked to be a statue of some kind. He got closer. It was carved out of an ancient pine, the torso of the man-shaped statue emerging right out of the trunk base. The arms of the statue were obviously once branches, stretching out to the sides and upwards with long fingers spreading out, made from the existing sub-branches. But what really got Doug was the face of the statue. It was a Bigfoot. It had deep-set eyes with a huge brow and a wide-open mouth with two huge rows of teeth. The carving was a stylized creation, and not the most realistic rendition ever, but it was clear as all hell what it was supposed to be. It definitely had a Native American look about it, reminding him of the artwork done in the Pacific Northwest by the Inuit cultures.

The carving was a totem. It had to be. It looked menacing. Its outstretched arms faced away from the valley as if to say: *Get the fuck out of here!* It was a spooky thing. The totem gave him the chills. Just looking at it made the hair on the back of his neck stand up. The Indians that originally lived here must have carved it, he thought. The tree looked ancient, like it was at least a couple of hundred years old, the bark dried and hardened from endless days in the sun.

So these things have been here a while, he thought. It was definitely odd, but then again, so was the whole situation. How could an animal this big hide from discovery for so long, at least from white people? Apparently the Indians knew about them and weren't exactly fond of them. *I know the feeling.*

Just then from deep in the valley, he heard a powerful roar. There was no doubt that the noise was made by the creature. The lung power on the Bigfoot was incredible. The creature's cry carried for miles. The bass levels were so low that Doug could feel the vibration in his chest. The sheer sound of it almost made him lose control. Yet this roar sounded different. It had a different tone to it. He thought it was the same animal, but it was more a long drawn out howl than a roar. The creature howled once more and a minute later, again. The valley was too dark and dense with trees for Doug to have the remotest chance of seeing anything. But one thing he could do was pinpoint the general direction of the source: somewhere a little southeast of where he stood, a quarter mile or so from a river at the bottom of the valley. He probably had another two hours or so of daylight left, so he started trudging down into the trees, determined to end this thing tonight.

Not long after, he noticed the smell. A pungent combination of garbage and body odor. The thing was close. He was ready for it this time. It was still too bright to sneak up on him now. He made circles continually looking around as he descended. Nothing showed and nothing moved. His ears couldn't make out anything. No birds, insects, nothing. Just the sound of his footfalls as he walked. The hairs raised on the back of his neck again. A stick broke on the ground behind him. He turned, aiming his rifle. There was nothing behind him. *Oh, this game again. Fine, I'll wait. I won't make the same mistake this time.* Doug would wait for it to come at him, and he would shoot it point blank this time. He would shoot it in the face. He would make sure he'd get it. He only had one shot, so he couldn't screw up.

The smell lingered, but there was no sign of anything. Doug had no choice but to continue towards the bottom of the valley, towards the original howls. It was damn near impossible to imagine that the creature could move through the forest that fast, especially without making any noise. It must have covered two miles in ten minutes after howling in the valley down below. Maybe it had become afraid of the shotgun. *It is probably waiting to attack me after dark. Shit. That makes sense,* Doug reasoned. It could tell from their encounter at the creek bed that Doug couldn't see at night. And last night was a new moon, so tonight was not going to offer much more light.

Doug heard the beast roar again, this time from the same general direction as the original howls at the bottom of the valley. It had that same long drawn out wail as the ones before. It howled again.

All the while Doug was making his way closer and closer to the bottom of the basin. He wasn't far now, probably a half-mile away from the source. *Keep howling,* he thought, *and I'll find you.* He moved at a quicker pace. It was only getting darker and this thing could easily blindside him from behind a tree, but for some reason his instincts told him to keep moving towards the source of that howling, like it would be an answer to his questions. He was tripping over logs that he wasn't seeing. Doug couldn't help it. He had not eaten in days and the sleep he had gotten was probably about an hour at best. Doug had never tested his endurance for this long and he felt like he could just drop at any moment.

He heard the howl again. *He was getting close,* he thought, *real close.* The trees were thinning up ahead. Doug could see holes in the canopy above him. He figured it was another hundred yards. The terrain started to take on a hilly feel, almost like ski moguls. He ran around them knowing he was so close. It was an odd place. It didn't look natural. The trees were clearing even more. Doug knew he was there. As a meadow opened up before him, Doug saw the strangest landscape he had ever seen. Amazement and horror washed over him. He had to be dreaming.

Pete Travers

CHAPTER FOURTEEN

Darrell, Evan and T-Bone reached the top of the
mountain pass. Nearing the top, they could hear the
howls in the valley on the other side. It made them
push harder, despite the pain in their lungs. Their
legs were cramping, but both men waited for the other
to quit first. Neither one wanted to stop. They arrived
at the top and saw the great basin below them, Doug's
clearly defined tracks leading right down into the
darkness of the lower elevations. They pushed on
immediately downhill, taking comfort in that the path
ahead lay on a much easier, downward slope. The dark
of night was coming fast now, the sun only touching
the very tips of the valley edges creating a pink ribbon
of color on the snow capped peaks along the far side of
the basin. They had very little time before nightfall.

Heading downward, they inevitably came within view
of the totem. As they neared the carved tree, Darrell
and Evan both were incredulous at the sight before
them. It rose up from the brush as they moved closer,

the grotesque shape silhouetted against the fiery backdrop of the setting sky. Although it was not clear to either man how the totem came into existence, it was clear what the totem was meant to represent. Its shape and features were unmistakable. Darrell had seen that face before, a long time ago.

"Jesus Christ, will you look at that!" Evan was aghast.

"Shit. I don't like the looks of this. This is some kind of keep away sign. We must not stay here long." Darrell had a very even tone about him, but he was visibly shaken. "If Doug is still down there, we must find him quickly."

"Why? What do you mean? Of course we have to find him quickly. Is there something you know about this carving?" Evan was confused by Darrell's behavior.

Darrell did not respond and stood motionless, staring at the tree carving.

Unfocused anger welled up inside Evan. "What do you know?!" he yelled.

"I don't know what I know!" Darrell turned and fired back. It was the first time either man had raised their voices at each other. "It's not my tribe. My reservation is hundreds of miles from here. But I can tell you that this..." Darrell pointed at the totem, "...is here for a reason!"

Evan's anger towards Darrell quickly subsided but his

frustration did not dissipate. Seeing the fear in Darrell's face incited a deep unnerving feeling inside Evan's mind that he could not shake.

Darrel tried to explain his train of thought. "Do you remember how I told you that these things could be nomadic?"

"Yeah."

"Well, why would the local people have a totem warding you away from a particular area if these creatures were typically elusive and did not like to be found?"

"I don't get it, Darrell. What's your point?"

"My point is: how badly are you willing to save your friend?" Darrell asked in a quiet tone.

Any sense of adrenaline that Evan possessed quickly washed away from his body. The way Darrell had asked the question stopped Evan in his tracks. Darrell was looking him right in the eyes, forcing Evan to truly think about what Darrell was asking.

"Are you willing to risk your life?" Darrel asked.

The weight of Darrell's question hit him hard and in a way that he was not prepared to answer. The two men stared at each other under the watchful eyes of the fearsome totem. A moment passed without either man speaking.

Darrell continued. "This is it, Evan. I know Doug is your friend, but there would be no shame in waiting here for the rest of the search party so that we have more protection."

Evan stared off into the direction of valley basin. "They would be too late and you know it."

"Probably. But without them we might all die. Doug might already be dead." Darrell returned.

"You do not know what's down there." Evan spat.

"You are right. I don't know. But I can sense it and I think you can too. There is great danger in this valley."

Evan stood there for a minute and attempted to weigh his choices. The preposterous nature of the situation trickled away into a harder reality. Sasquatch was real, and it was down in the valley. Doug was down in the valley, alone. Those were the realities that came to haunt him. Evan wondered what his life would be worth if he left Doug alone in the woods to die. It was too difficult to imagine living a day beyond this point without remembering that he abandoned his friend when he needed Evan the most. If Evan did not try, his decision would haunt him until the day he died. He had much of his life left, but it would be at too high of a cost.

"I am going down there." Evan finally responded.

For a moment, Darrell was quiet with his eyes closed. He then opened his eyes and stared at the gnarled tree before him. "I am going with you."

"Thank you." Evan gratefully acknowledged. Evan's determination was well founded in his friendship for Doug, but Darrell was a stranger to both men until two days ago. Evan could only think that Darrell was a man of high virtue and great courage to risk his life in this way.

"Get your shotgun ready, Evan. Make sure you are fully loaded and you can reload quickly if needed."

"C'mon T-Bone! Let's go find Doug!" Evan released his anxiety on T-Bone, dragging her down the hill. She was whimpering but they needed her to follow the scent. Darrell had one last look at the totem, took a deep breath and followed the other two into the dark valley.

Doug's fear was making him sick to his stomach. He peered around in a complete circle. It was as if a veil had been dropped from his eyes, revealing a scene to him he had not seen before. He was still surrounded by the large mound foundations, yet these mounds were slightly different. The ones before looked like mossy earthen hills, covered in vegetation. But these new ones were covered with larger rocks, with no vegetation upon them.

These mounds were newer.

Doug was surrounded by dozens of the rock formations. The rock-strewn mounds were waist high, some over fifteen feet in length. All of them covered in rocks. All around him. And beyond those, were hundreds of other earthen mounds as far as the eye could see through the trees. These were not geological formations. These were made, built for a purpose. The word that came to mind was "man-made", but that didn't apply here, for no man had made these. Any other man would have come here and thought otherwise, but Doug knew differently. No other man had followed a Bigfoot into this area, and heard a Bigfoot howling into the sky. The long drawn out howling he had heard when he was at the ridge made sense now. Everything made sense now. The Bigfoot wasn't howling, it was mourning.

These are graves. Bigfoot graves. They bury their dead.

It had finally made sense to him. All the time Doug had been trailing the creature, he didn't know where it was going, but now he understood. It was going to bury its son where they all must be buried. Buried in a sacred place, a place of hiding.

That's why the Bigfoot had attacked him by the creek bed. That was why it had chased him into the rapids. It was scaring him away, so that he would not find this place. That's what the totem was for. The totem was meant to scare anybody away who might venture into the valley.

Doug was starting to get an understanding of how intelligent these creatures were, a whole species of animal, living under our very noses, living here for probably longer than we had been here, in total secrecy from man.

The Bigfoot had come here to bury its son.

As Doug wandered aimlessly through the giant mounds, he came upon a smaller one, not nearly as high and as long as the others. But it looked brand new, with fresh dirt and rocks loosely piled on top. This was probably where the young one had been buried. Doug looked at the formation. Only then, after days of being out in the woods alone, did he ponder what he had truly done. He had killed the Bigfoot's son. Now the parallels were coming clear to him. Was attacking Chad an act of revenge? A son for a son. Had the Bigfoot witnessed the killing of it's own son and exacted vengeance upon the son of the murderer? That's what it was. It was murder. He had murdered another being. Doug felts pangs of guilt even though he knew his act was accidental, or unintentional. Doug did shoot the gun, but he had thought he was shooting a bear.

Doug's concentration shifted to the growing sounds around him. He could hear them. *Yes, them,* Doug thought. Not one. Many.

Evan and Darrell were plowing through the brush down the incline of the valley. The mood had changed drastically for the two men since finding the totem. Now there was fear, a building apprehension for their own lives. Both men could feel it. Neither man had really felt any strong sense of self-peril through the miles of forest that they had traveled. But now, they were trudging right into the very heart of danger. The whole valley had an air about it, a great sense of foreboding. There were no sounds from the forest around them, no birds, no wind, nothing. The only sound was just their own, extremely noisy, footsteps crashing through the vegetation. The men could sense that their clamorous footfalls were like an alarm to some unseen onlookers, beyond the edge of their vision. But they could not do anything about it. They were out of time.

The shadows were coming closer. Night was nearly there. Doug could see very little, but he could see the dark apparitions moving at the edges of his vision. Doug thought of how he had miraculously survived that night by the riverbed, of how that thing could have killed him at any moment. Yet somehow, he had managed to live. The sasquatch did not want to kill him, only break him, break his resolve from following him here. This valley was a secret place, a place where no man was ever supposed to be. But *he* was here. Doug was in the very heart of it. They were circling him now, grunts and angry growls from the edges of his eyesight. Doug was in a forbidden place, and he was caught in a trap.

They were not going to let him out alive.

Doug had his shotgun, but only one bullet shell. He considered that maybe he could shoot one of them, but what difference would that make? Piss them off even more? They were going kill him. He thought of how the animal had pulled his shoulder out. Did the creature know what it was doing? Was the creature's intention to hurt him so that he could not follow? Only this time, they were going to really pull him apart. Doug could run, but they would certainly catch him. A putrid stench was growing in the air. By the building sounds and smells around him, Doug could tell that the creatures were getting agitated. Trees were snapping and loud grunts came from shadows.

Then the big one yelled. Doug turned to his right and caught sight of the patriarch in mid-roar. He knew it was the father. Its roar was deafening, shaking the ground beneath him. Then the others yelled in turn all around him. The combined noise was so loud that in rang in Doug's ears. The weight of the uproar made Doug lose his balance and drop to his knees. He felt weak, afraid. Above all, he felt alone. The giant beings moved in closer, surrounding him. Doug did not want to die like this, but it had occurred to him that he deserved it. He had failed. He had failed Chad. Doug turned the shotgun around towards his face. With his hand still holding the trigger, he put his mouth around the end of the barrel. *If I am going to die, I am going to do it on my own terms,* Doug thought.

Darrell, Evan and T-Bone made it to the edge of the mounds. It was pure resolve that kept them going towards the roars ahead of them. Several times when they heard the roars of numerous creatures, they glanced at each other but said nothing. Both men now realized that there was more than one Bigfoot in this valley, possibly many more.

As they weaved their way through the earthen moguls, Evan was struck by the strange layout of mounds before them.

"What are these things?" Evan asked, referring to the mounds.

"You fully loaded?" Darrell asked.

"Yeah."

"Good. Start firing now! Fire into the air! Don't stop until we find him!" The two men, with the dog in tow sprinted through the formations. They fired their shotguns into the air, screaming for Doug. The woods around them were alive. Giant shadows drifted through the gaps in the trees. They were moving so fast, that if only one of the animals were to step in their way, they would have run right into it. Their only hope was that the noise from the shotgun blasts was enough to keep their would-be assailants at bay.

"C'mon Doug! Call back!" Darrell screamed, pleading between breaths. Then he remembered what Forsythe had told him about Chad.

Doug heard a shotgun blast and thought himself dead. But then more blasts went off. Were those echoes in his dreams? He did not feel dead. Yet there was blackness around him. Doug was not sure if the darkness was the emptiness of death or the black of night. Then he heard a voice. It was distant, but was getting louder, as if it was approaching him.

It sounded like someone had said *Chad*. He'd heard it. It was faint, but distinct. Doug was going to see Chad again.

"Chad's OK! Chad's OK! Doug, answer me!" a distant voice cried.

The sounds were getting closer. The volume of noise came crashing into his awareness. The howls, the screams, the shotgun blasts. Something was looming over him. Someone. *Chad? Is that you? I am sorry.*

Darrell and Evan reached the clearing. Looking back on it, Darrell later determined that the most frightening vision of his childhood had been replaced by what he saw now. A circle of giant hairy humanoids, the creatures Darrell had known to be the Yeahoh, were surrounding a man on his knees in the middle. It was Doug Childress. He looked so small compared to the encroaching monsters. Doug was holding the end of a shotgun in his mouth.

"Doug! It's me, Evan!" Evan shouted as loud as he could, reloading and firing again and again.

Standing in front of Doug was the largest of giant creatures. It must have been ten feet tall and massively built. The great humanoid was covered in short matted hair from head to toe, except on its face. The face was black as coal, and was absent of light except for bright glints from its two dark orbs.

"Chad is OK! Chad is OK! We know you're innocent! Doug! Snap out of it! Everything is all right!"

The creatures seemed spurred on by the sight of the new humans entering the clearing. The angry mob of beasts was not pleased by the presence of these new intruders, and they turned to face Darrell and Evan. They beat their chests and screamed at the new arrivals. The patriarch did not however, and stayed focused on the human at its feet. Darrell, with his free hand, grabbed his flashlight and shined it on Doug, casting a pale glow on the creatures immediately around him. Darrell could clearly see the patriarch now. The big one had its arms raised above Doug, ready to crush the life out of him.

Doug was drifting out of his dream state. He was
starting to recognize the voices around him. One of the
voices was unmistakably Evan, and the other sounded
like the sheriff that had arrested him. They were the
ones speaking about Chad. *What were they saying?
Chad is OK? Chad is alive?* It did not make any sense.
Doug did not know what had happened to him, but he
knew that he was still alive.

His coherence had completely returned, and from
Darrell's flashlight beam, he could see what stood
before him. Its chest was heaving; its muscles flexing.
Its two great arms clasped together at the hands to
form a giant hammer. The face of the creature showed
pure aggression.

The shotguns were blaring repeatedly from both
Darrell and Evan. The creatures were swirling around
Doug in a wild frenzy. Their motions revealed a
strange behavior. Their intensity was increasing,
indicating the tension mounting towards Doug and the
giant sasquatch. On the surface, the scene resembled
pure chaos, but the wild behavior belied a deliberate
communication amongst the creatures. It was as if
they were urging the great one to complete the task
and kill the small human at their feet.

"They are not backing away!" Darrell screamed.

"Should I shoot the big one?!" Evan asked Darrell
between blasts into the air.

"Wait." Darrell needed to clear his head. He didn't think they could take the big one down in one shot, and then what? What if they hurt it, but it could still move? The Yeahoh could then charge the men in mass and take them down. Then they would all most assuredly die. But they had to do something fast. Otherwise, they would run out of ammunition and not be able to get any closer to Doug. It was a stalemate that the men would lose. They had to take a new course of action. Darrell reasoned that the only way to get Doug out of the tightening noose was to get the creatures to back away on their own accord. Shooting into the air was not working. Killing one of the smaller creatures would not help either.

"Evan, listen to me!" Darrell got Evan's attention through the shotgun volleys. "Shoot a smaller one… in the leg. Hurt it but don't kill it. Make sure that the big one sees you. We want to draw attention away from Doug. Can you do that?"

"What if it comes after me?" Evan asked not out of fear for his own life, but to know what his next course of action needed to be. He could see as well, that shooting into the air was not getting them anywhere.

"Then shoot it again." Darrell firmly responded.

With little hesitation, Evan lowered his shotgun horizontally, took aim and fired at one of the smaller creatures immediately surrounding Doug. The animal took the shotgun blast right in the thigh. Both of its hands went to the wound, and it grimaced in pain.

But it did not go down.

Evan kept his vision and his shotgun targeted on the wounded creature, but yelled over to Darrell. "Didn't work!"

"Shoot it again! Take it down, but don't kill it!" Darrell yelled.

Evan fired again. The bullet penetrated the same thigh, only a few inches higher. The creature was screaming in pain, but it did not go down. The others were taking notice, and getting angrier by the second.

"Now, how is this a good idea?" Evan asked over his shoulder to Darrell with his rifle still aimed at the creature. Evan was amazed at the power of the Bigfoot to withstand two shotgun blasts, and this was one of the smaller ones.

"Shoot it again." Darrell returned.

This time Evan hesitated. All of the creatures looked like they were going to attack them in a rush. They were all facing Evan now. Some were crouching lower with their arms out wide. There was no way that the two men could fend them all off if the creatures charged at the same time. Doubt of Darrell's plan crept into Evan's mind, but Evan could not think of anything else to try.

The twice-shot Bigfoot limped forward towards the helpless form of Doug, still slumped on the ground.

Instead of retreating, the beast chose to attack, lifting its arms above its head, ready to strike Doug down. Evan noted that the creatures' resolve was startling. He could not let the humanoid get to his friend. Evan lifted the shotgun sight to his eye, took aim for the creature's wounded leg and fired. A blast of meat and blood issued from the monster's tattered thigh. The creature went down on its back as it writhed in pain. It did not return to its feet.

The big one took notice this time. Its hands still locked over its head like a great hammer, but its eyes were upon the wounded Bigfoot. It then turned towards the two hunters.

The two men inched closer, closer to Doug, closer to the circle. Darrell's fear was absolute. His childhood memories had scarred him for life, and now to be walking towards a group of angry Yeahoh was practically unbearable. He had never crossed this far into facing his fears. The Yeahoh were everything that his memories made them out to be. Monsters. And they were real. And they wanted to kill him.

Doug pulled his shotgun from his mouth and aimed it at the giant Bigfoot in front of him. The creature's coal black eyes dropped to meet Doug's. Doug had one shell left and now was his opportunity to get a clear shot at point blank range. But Doug knew he couldn't kill the creature. What was disturbing Doug's battle weary mind was that he found that he did not want to kill it. He just wanted to get away. He pointed the gun at its chest and slowly pushed away, lying on his back with his feet digging in the ground, finding traction where he could in the soft dirt.

The other men continued to fire away, now into the air again, edging slowly closer to Doug. Seeing one of their brethren get hurt by the shotgun blasts, the volleys into the air now held meaning for the angry creatures. The circle around Doug had finally parted. Evan continued to fire, as Darrell made a move to pull Doug out. Darrell grabbed Doug under his arm and leaned back to gain leverage. As Darrell came within close range of the creatures, he was affronted by the pungent stench. The sheriff managed to drag Doug a few yards away from the circle of creatures, but it was difficult, especially with one arm.

"Doug, it's me, Darrell. Can you understand me?!" Darrell pleaded.

"Yeah, ... I'm here." Doug half-grunted back.

"Do you need ammo?"

"Uh ...yeah."

Darrell put his own shotgun under his arm to free his hand, and then pulled a handful of shells from his coat pocket and tossed them to Doug, all the while monitoring the animals around him. It seemed that they were waiting to jump on him as soon as he got distracted. He had to stay focused. The creatures had the upper hand and there were too many to kill. He dropped the shotgun back into his hand.

The three men backed slowly away from the circle of giant humanoids, their guns pointed at the group. They put more than twenty yards of distance between themselves before the Bigfoots started to change their behavior. The circle slowly dispersed into the shadows of the woods, almost instantly departing from view. Only the patriarch remained in view, unmoving, staring at Doug. Darrell's flashlight still cast its pale yellow beam on the face of the great beast. Its expression was perplexing and frightening at the same time. It held its ceaseless gaze on the man who had chased it for so long. Doug could not understand what the creature's visage meant. It was not anger, but something else - something beyond a simple emotion like anger.

But there was no time to ponder the meaning behind the patriarch's fixed stare. The other creatures had entered the cover of the deep woods. Evan noticed the noises behind him almost immediately. The creatures were starting to circle around the group of men.

"Uhh, guys? We had better start moving a lot faster!" Evan blurted.

Darrell understood Evan's concern. "Form a line! Evan! Take the back! I'll lead us out." Darrell screamed at Doug, practically kicking him into action. "Doug, watch our sides! Move!"

Their progress was painfully slow as they marched out of the valley. Moving away from the clearing, the forest tightened around them once more. They had only one flashlight, so they couldn't shine in front and in back at the same time. Darrell decided to shine the light forward, to illuminate the path before them. The guttural sounds from the darkness were now to the sides and behind them. For the moment, it seemed that the men had avoided being outflanked, but the sasquatches were not far behind. Doug and Evan were left to firing randomly, following the sounds. They weren't firing into the air anymore, but aiming directly into the woods around them. The foliage blasted away as the gunshots roared into the dark forest around them.

The creatures were building into a frenzy, and the only thing that was keeping them from charging was the sting of the shotgun blasts. Their frantic screams echoed back, but the Yeahoh did not stop coming at them. Darting in and out of the shadows, the creatures used the valley's dense foliage for protection. They were gaining on the men. It seemed only a matter of time.

Suddenly, a large rock flew from the darkness and struck Evan. Pain shot through his left arm, and he went down. Evan fired point blank, straight up as a Bigfoot rushed over and past him. Darrell turned back, aimed and shot the creature in the chest as it turned to attack again. The blast knocked the creature down and back into the brush. Doug helped Evan back to his feet, and then he turned back, firing in a strafing pattern. With so many creatures in the vicinity, Doug felt like he couldn't miss. But the creatures were not being subdued. They kept coming at them in relentless pursuit.

Darrell had never been more scared in his entire life. Gone from his mind were all of the priorities in his life. His family, his career, everything that had shaped his life up until this point, had been rendered unimportant. Only the need for survival remained. Darrell had not considered himself a religious man, not in the ways of his people, and he suddenly felt regret for that spiritual choice. The attack upon him now by the Great Ones felt like a punishment. Punished for turning away from the old ways, was Darrell to be killed by those spirits which his people revered? But even though he had become distant from his tribal customs, he did not forget them. Darrell resorted to chanting in the old tongue, warding off the evil spirits as he charged ahead.

Doug's mood had changed considerably. The events around him were happening so quickly, he barely had enough time keep his mind on moving forward. But Chad was alive. These men, who now knew that Bigfoot was not just a myth, were here to help him. And they were all in great danger. It wasn't about himself anymore. He could not have gone on living with Chad's death, but the shame of Chad was now coupled with concern for his best friend and this sheriff. He knew they must have risked a lot to be here.

The stench was practically unbearable, with the creatures all around them. Deep in the shadows, large branches were being snapped in two.

Minutes seemed like hours. The men were slowly, but surely, running out of ammunition. They had brought enough for a manhunt, but not a war. In an effort to stretch their resources, they reduced the frequency of their shotgun blasts. But the inevitable came to pass.

"I'm out!" Evan cried as he clenched his shotgun. He didn't know whether he should face forward so that he could move faster or turn around and walk backwards so that he could see his assailants. Either choice seemed like a bad idea.

"I'm out, too!" Darrell followed. Not having the shotgun blasts to clear a path made things go from bad to horrible.

Doug, with one shell left, fired right over Darrell's shoulder in the direction in front of them. Whether it did anything or not to clear the way, it gave them the courage to keep moving forward, for another few yards at least.

And then, with forest still ahead of them, they were completely out of ammunition. They had no way to defend themselves.

Before, the three men had moved at a quick but measured pace. Now they ran as fast as they could. T-Bone took the lead, growling and barking, determining a path through the trees. The creatures, noticing the lack of shotgun blasts, were getting bolder now. Evan could hear the breathing of one not ten feet behind him. It was only a matter of time before one would pull him down. The men sprinted through the brush, screaming incoherently, all of them. Inevitably, they were all running side by side, needing to watch the flashlight to maintain the speed that they were moving through the foliage. One trip now and it would be all over.

And then, straight in front of them, twenty feet away, stood a creature. Not the biggest, but still well over six feet and full of girth. It was blocking their path, probably hoping to corral the men as the other creatures came at them from the sides. They were trapped. It was over.

But then T-Bone growled in a low guttural tone and leaped right at the man-beast in front of them.

The animal caught the bloodhound in mid-leap and they both went down in a tumble. The men rushed past the melee, all hoping that T-Bone had enough strength to get away. To stop and help her would only have resulted in their own deaths. Thirty yards past, they could hear the painful yelp of a dog.

"T-Bone?!" Evan cried. He paused, which made the other men pause. Evan wanted to turn back and go kill that thing. He couldn't believe that T-Bone would sacrifice herself like that.

Darrell grabbed Evan by the arm hard and yanked him back to his senses. "You're not going to be able to save her! Let's go!" Darrell roughly pushed him along.

And then they were into the clear at the valley ridge.
They passed by the totem. Running with every last bit
of energy over the snow-covered ground, the three
crossed over the ridge into the pass. The howls from
the valley behind them continued. It felt like the land
itself was angry with them. The vengeful cries kept
them running even downhill, to the point where their
footfalls were more like leaps, as the angle of the
mountain maintained its steepness. Down the
mountain they fell, trying to put as much ground
between them and the valley as possible. Doug fell face
forward, landing awkwardly and painfully wrenching
his shoulder again. He had to ignore it and get up.
Stabbing pain told him he had dislocated it again, but
he could not stop to tend to it. It would have to be put
back in later. The scene was a tumbling mass of
bodies and snow, each man feeling the same thing.

They had cheated death.

Pete Travers

CHAPTER FIFTEEN

Gaining their footing at the bottom of the snowline,
Evan braced Doug while Darrell lifted his arm and
popped Doug's shoulder back in. Doug let out a gasp
of pain as his bone fell back into the socket. Waves of
nausea rolled over him, while the two watched him
recover from the initial burst of pain. Once Doug
showed signs that the pain had subsided, they urged
him to start moving again. They quickly continued
downward along the sloping earth at the base of the
mountain range. In any other situation, they would
have let the man rest but the thought of those
creatures barreling down the mountain after them was
enough to keep anybody moving. Doug did not argue
and ambled along, cradling his arm.

An hour passed with no sounds of pursuit from the
dark woods around them. A steady mist came down
from the starless sky, heralding rainfall. The moisture
crept into their clothes, and soon the men were
shivering in the chilled and damp night air.

After putting more than two miles between themselves and the mountaintop, they could hear something making its way down the hillside behind them. They still held their shotguns, but they were more like clubs than guns at this point, being completely out of ammunition. Hopefully the creatures could not sense that they were defenseless, but they did not know what to think anymore. The footfalls got closer and closer, and then they heard the familiar panting of a dog. A bloodhound emerged from the dark ground brush.

"T-Bone!" Evan went over to hug the dog, feeling grateful after thinking he was never going to see her again. T-Bone quickly rubbed up against Evan and licked his face, but then abruptly broke from his hug and continued moving forward, away from the mountains. She was noticeably limping, but still very mobile. The dog clearly did not want to linger here, and neither did they, so they quickly followed. *Smart dog,* Doug thought.

Onward they marched, not talking, saving their breath, guided by the dim glow of Darrell's flashlight. It was raining heavily now. Being back on the western side of the mountains, they were traveling directly into the storm. The rainfall had drenched the men completely, soaking through all of their layers of clothing.

A dense tree-line appeared again, and T-Bone moved ahead into it, disappearing into the trees. Evan was not concerned. T-Bone would figure out her way back to camp, and she didn't need anybody's help to do it. They were the ones that needed help, especially Doug. Having been without food for days, Doug could feel a wobbliness in his muscles, his legs shaking just trying to support himself. He focused on the beam from Darrell's flashlight, moving forward in a trance-like state.

And then in an instant, Doug saw Darrell's flashlight swing away to the left. Something rushed by Doug with blinding speed. Doug heard Evan make a grunting noise as he was hit hard by something. Evan was launched into the brush some ten yards from where he was originally standing. It happened fast, without any warning. The speed was terrifying. Doug tried to lift his shotgun, but it was ripped out of his hands. Through the dim cloud light he could see that something huge stood before him, a massive man-like shadow barely silhouetted against the sky. It immediately grabbed Doug by the head, its palm covering Doug's face, and its giant fingers wrapping around the shape of his head. He had no choice but to grab the monster's huge forearm and hang on as he was raised fully three feet off the ground. Doug could see through the gaps between the creature's fingers. The giant beast's strength was immeasurable. Doug tried to writhe around, hopefully to shake the thing's grip. Yet the arm did not move. Not at all. He might as well have been trying to bend a steel girder. A moment passed and nothing happened.

Darrell, taken out at the legs, was conscious but not

mobile. He knew the shotgun was somewhere nearby, but he couldn't retrieve it unless it was within his immediate reach. Without ammunition, it could only be used as a club. Without being able to use his legs, he couldn't do much of anything to help Doug. He grabbed the flashlight and aimed it at the Bigfoot, pointing it at the creature's eyes, doubtfully hoping to blind it.

Doug could see the animal's face as the rain-specked beam illuminated the creature from the side. It didn't even turn towards Darrell's direction as the bright beam struck its face. It just kept staring at Doug, rain landing on its face and hair. Doug was all the giant humanoid seemed to be focused on. Doug began to realize that this was not just an instinctive animal. It could have killed any of them easily, for it had dispatched Darrell and Evan in mere seconds, with little effort. But it seemed to have only disabled the other two men, making the conscious decision to not kill them.

It was only really after Doug.

All it wanted now was revenge, Doug thought. An eye for an eye. A death for a death. It lifted Doug at a higher angle up to the night sky. The beast's chest heaved out as air filled its great lungs, and it let go a wild roar. The bellow was louder than any of them had heard before. There was only sound now. Only the loud blast of the creature's howl.

Darrell could not do anything but stare at the creature

holding Doug high into the air, dwarfing him like he was a small child. The creature continued to hold Doug, with its arm straight away from its body, its giant hand wrapped completely around Doug's face and head. The strength that the giant humanoid was exhibiting was awesome. Doug seemed so fragile. One quick rotation from the animal's shoulder and Doug's neck would be broken. That same feeling of helplessness came over Darrell as when he was a boy at the lodge. He just sat there and watched, his arm shaking, locked into position with the flashlight beam shining on the horrific scene in front of him.

Doug knew it was the same Bigfoot, the same one that had attacked him by the riverbed. The same creature that had chased him into the rapids. The same one that was going to crush him at the graveyard. The same one whose son he had shot.

Before, Doug was spurned on by rage, revenge for Chad's life. But now he knew that Chad was alive. He was not on equal ground with the creature anymore. He had kept his son but this thing's child was dead. He looked into the creature's one visible eye, the other cast in shadow. It was looking at him in a way that he could not understand. There was emotion there, but he didn't know what. It was not anger, nor sadness, but just a cold penetrating stare, alluding to some resolute incomprehensible emotion. The look triggered Doug into thinking that this thing could have taken them all out any time it wanted. It was as if all of its actions were calculated decisions. The beast had intelligence. Doug could feel it.

This creature, so powerful, could not have tried to kill Chad and failed. It was impossible. The creature had intended to let Chad live. Seeing its son get attacked, through the anguish it surely felt, the creature acted in a manner that was not without mercy. Mercy, from an animal. And Doug had been tracking this animal through this forest, its home, hoping to take the remains of its son and use it as evidence. Fear was replaced by shame.

Doug, with a black-skinned giant hand pressed against his face, awkwardly mouthed the words: "I am sorry."

The creature's chiseled face did not move. It did not even blink. Its black orbs continued to penetrate Doug's mind, bombarding his psyche by ripping away the layers of lies he had told himself. The creature's son's death was his fault. Chad getting hurt was his fault. His divorce was his fault. So much of his life that he deferred blame for was his fault. His life felt shallow and weak.

And then creature dropped Doug. He fell in a heap, his knees giving way. Doug landed hard on his back. He stared straight up and the creature, so tall, was still within his vision. It took one huge leap right over him, and then with another stride it was into the forest and gone.

Doug continued to stare straight up, the rain dropping straight down at him from a dark indiscernible sky. Moments passed.

Darrell crawled towards Doug, asking if he was all right. Doug did not speak but nodded his head. He sat up and helped Darrell to his feet. Darrell could tell that his thigh was not broken, but he was probably going to have a massive contusion in the morning.

They found Evan in the bushes, groaning and slowly returning to consciousness. Evan looked relieved when he saw the other men come to his aid.

"Did I miss anything?" Evan asked in a drunken tone. It wasn't lightheartedness, but rather an emotion revealing incredulousness when the situation gets so surreal and traumatic that it becomes absurd. Darrell couldn't help but laugh even in tremendous pain. But Doug wasn't showing any emotion. Darrell thought that Doug might be in shock. Doug had been through more trauma in the past three days than most people go through in their entire lives, and he was bound to fall apart. But Doug just continued to wear a strange, silent expression.

The reality of their situation was coming back to Darrell. "We'd better get going. We are at least a few hours from the search party or the camp and we have no ammunition. We will not survive if that thing comes back."

"It won't be coming back." Doug responded in a quiet

even tone. Darrell and Evan both turned and looked at him curiously.

"It's done with us. It's done with me." Doug stated.

A silent communication passed between Darrell and Evan and they knew somehow that Doug was speaking the truth. Darrell knew now that Doug was not in shock, for he understood Doug's calm expression. It was gratefulness.

Just then T-Bone appeared in the clearing, her head hung low in a *bad dog* pose.

Evan reassured her, "It's OK girl, I'd have been long gone if I were you." and patted her side.

Doug knew that Evan was not telling the truth. "No you wouldn't have, because you didn't leave. You two risked your lives to save me, and I will never forget that. Thank you."

After a moment, Darrell spoke. "In my tribe, we had a saying for when a person survived a life-threatening experience. Naheo ch' ce'xhew's ch'un'. It means: now you begin the rest of your life."

Doug nodded and thought about what that meant to him. "I want to see my son."

"I bet you do." Darrell returned.

"Let's go." Doug stated as he put Darrell's arm over his

shoulders to help him. Evan managed to get to his
feet. Doug then led the way at a slow but steady pace
towards the camp. It felt good to be helping someone
else for a change.

They wandered on, back the way they had come. The
night passed as the rain clouds slowly dissipated,
followed by the clearing of the gray front to reveal
splashes of welcome morning sun. With the events
from the past, the three men all felt that the danger
was behind them and now they had to just make it
home. They had made it. But Doug had something
else nagging at his thoughts. He paused in his tracks
and spoke.

"None of us will ever mention anything about this
place to anyone,...ever." He said it in such a quiet tone
but it was a resolute one. Something had changed in
Doug, a calmness that he felt, like for once in his life,
he absolutely knew he was doing the right thing.
Maybe, someday, others would find the valley and
make it known to the world. The discoverers would
become famous, and the valley would be inevitably and
irrevocably changed forever. Changed only for the
worse. Scientists and anthropologists would pour into
the No Return from all over the world, and they would
need protection from the very creatures they chose to
study. The enigmatic creatures would fiercely protect
their valley, as they must have for centuries. Even
with the best of intentions, destruction of the habitat
would occur. But for now, Doug had decided, the

valley would remain a secret. At least for a little while longer.

 "Agreed… and don't ask me for any more ideas for what to do on long weekends anymore." Evan pleaded.

"Agreed." Darrell said. Darrell realized, however, that if that were to be the way things would stay, something had to be done about Doug's story.

CHAPTER SIXTEEN

In three long but almost peaceful hours, the three men and the dog made it to the rain-soaked clearing where the grizzly bear had been killed. By now the flies and mosquitoes were swarming over the giant kill. Doug and Evan barely gave the carcass a second look, wanting to move on and get home. But Darrcll paused at the kill, a thought coming to him. Evan was about to ask Darrell what was wrong, but the sheriff spoke first.

"We're staying here." Darrell stated.

Evan was about to ask why, but Doug, who had guessed what Darrell was thinking, responded with a quiet: "Thank you."

"You're welcome Doug. It will take quite a bit to convince the doctor of this, but I'll make sure that it happens. You have my word."

"What's going on?" Evan asked, totally confused.

"Doug's story of an animal attacking his son is going to stick, but it's going to be a different animal than we have been after. I only wish we had more ammunition so that the bear could look like it had been shot."

"What are you two talking about?" Evan pleaded as he watched the other two men gaze over at the bear carcass. Evan put it all together and then nodded in recognition. "Do you think it will fly?" Evan asked.

"I am going to make it fly." The sheriff responded. He picked up his radio and gave it a try. A crackling voice came over the speaker. It was Forsythe.

Darrell relayed his basic position as best he could, based on his surroundings. "We're a couple miles west of the mountains in a large clearing. We are just below the timberline. If you have followed our trail, you'll run right into us. How long will it take to get here?"

"Affirmative sheriff, we have your trail, although it was difficult in the rain, but we should be there within the hour." Forsythe indicated.

Darrell responded. "Good. We have Childress and the animal that attacked his son. We will wait here for you." Darrell turned off the radio as he looked at Doug.

"Thank you again, sheriff." Doug stated.

Forsythe and his team made for the area where the sheriff designated. He noticed that it followed the straight course that they had pursued for miles. It was not long before the dogs had picked up the scent of a dead animal and the pace quickened. Through the water saturated terrain they went, until they came to a large glade. Forsythe was not sure what he was expecting, but he was very surprised by what unfolded before him.

Three men stood in the center of the clearing, their clothes tattered and muddied. A bloodhound dog waited patiently next to one man that he guessed to be Evan Ratcliffe. And before the men lay the huge carcass of a giant grizzly bear. Forsythe did not know what to think of the sheriff's radio message, stating Childress and the animal had been found. Were they not one and the same? The answers came to him as he saw the giant mound of fur and meat on the clearing floor. Something did not seem right about the situation in Forsythe's mind. It was as if they had found the last missing piece to the puzzle, but it was not the right fit. But since it was the last piece, it had to fit. Still, Forsythe had the nagging sensation that something wasn't quite right.

"So, who killed it?" Forsythe asked as he gazed upon the bug-infested mound.

"Yeah deputy, everybody's all right. Thanks for

asking." Darrell fired out in biting sarcasm. He knew that if this was going to work, he was going to have to get Forsythe to behave properly. He needed the search party to see the carcass but also to move on quickly. With a simple inspection, it would have been easy to realize that the bear had not been killed by bullet wounds.

"Well it's going to be difficult to do an autopsy on the bear…" Forsythe began.

Darrell cut him off, feigning a temper. "Jesus Christ, Forsythe! No one is going to run an autopsy on the fucking bear, twenty miles into the woods. With the distance we are going to have to hike today, it's going to be hard enough to get back before nightfall. And we are not going to let this man wait out here another minute." He pointed to Doug. "He's been through enough, and it wouldn't have been that way if we had believed his story in the fucking first place! What's the matter with you?!"

The words stung Forsythe. Something did not sit right in his mind, but he was overwhelmed by the sheriff's outburst. He had never seen the sheriff raise his voice like that. Anger welled up inside of him, feeling the shame at being lectured in front of the large group. Darrell limped up to him and past him, readying to take control of the party, but then he fell to his knees, clutching his leg. Forsythe was forced to come to his aid, leading him away from the clearing. Forsythe lifted him up and put the sheriff's arm over his shoulder.

"Thank you Forsythe." The sheriff stated through winces. "Sorry about my temper. We are just all tired. Let's get out of here."

Forsythe had no response other than to nod his head. Thousands of questions swirled around in his brain. He still could not shake the nagging sensation that something was amiss, but the sheriff did not seem to want anything but to get out of there. He wanted to stop and ask more questions of the situation, but it meant defiance to his superior. Forsythe acquiesced and let the sheriff lean on him for support as the search party ambled away from the clearing.

Doug looked at the sheriff and silently acknowledged him for what he had done. He looked back at the giant Sawtooth Mountains behind him. Their foreboding visage was a grim reminder of what lay beyond. One last look and Doug turned forward to follow the already moving search party. It was time to move on. It was time to see his son. It was time to begin the rest of his life.

High in the woods, with a clear view of the glade below, the giant being observed the small human that had followed it through the forest for so long. It could see the man turn towards its direction. The man paused for a moment and then moved to join the rest of the men gathered at the far edge of the clearing. The creature watched the group of humans and dogs meander away. As they moved out of earshot, the great Omah headed north, following the ridge of mountains into the higher, more remote recesses of the No Return.

Acknowledgements

I would like to thank my wife, Kelly Travers, for the editing and publishing of this book. As well her contributions to character and plot design are not only invaluable, they are essential to the narrative. This book is as much hers as it is mine.

About the Author

Pete Travers, by day, works
as a Visual Effects Supervisor
on motion pictures. His film
credits include such films as
*The Aviator, Matrix: Reloaded,
The Two Towers, Harry Potter
and the Sorcerer's Stone,* and
What Dreams May Come.

Pete is also involved in bigfoot research, speaking with
numerous individuals who claim to have seen the
creature. Pete has worked with eyewitnesses and has
produced a compilation of sketches, which will be
released to the public soon.

This is Pete's first novel.

Pete lives with his wife, Kelly, in Santa Barbara,
California.